I0685388

LOVE AT HAILEY'S COMET

BY

Kimberly A. Biggerstaff

This novella is a work of fiction. Names, characters, businesses, organizations, places, events, and incidents other than those clearly in the public domain are either the product of the author's imagination or, if real, used in a fictitious manner. Where real-life historical persons appear, the situations, incidents, and dialogues concerning those persons are entirely fictional and are not intended to depict actual events or to change the entirely fictional nature of the work. In all other respects, any resemblance to persons living or dead is entirely coincidental.

Cover design by Kimberly Biggerstaff using www.canva.com.

Novels by Kimberly A. Biggerstaff

A Rogov Romance

Lex's Story

Lex's Story Part II: Life Unguarded

Love at the Pentagon: A Nick & Gia Story

Other novellas and novels by Alex A. Jameson (Kimberly A.

Biggerstaff)

The Sam Barrett Ops

Operation: Running Brook

Operation: Russian Roulette

Operation: Returning Home

Operation: Rising Son

Operation: Payback

Operation: Rescue Requited

Operation: Birdwatcher

Operation: Cougar

Kimberly A. Biggerstaff © 2024

Contents

AUTHOR'S NOTE:

Sam Barrett is not the main character of this novella. However she does play a part, and for context, this novella takes place sometime between *Operation: Returning Home* and *Operation: Rising Son* (Books 3 and 4) of the series *The Sam Barrett Ops*.

CHAPTER 1

Alexandra Yates added another ten-pound plate to each side of the bar. Replacing the clamps, she grabbed her water bottle and took a swig. She walked to the center of the bar and prepared herself while lining her shins up to touch the cool steel. She took a deep breath and then hinged at the hips. Keeping her back straight and using the "over and under" grip, she grabbed the bar. Bending her knees while ensuring a straight back, she lifted the weight, running it along her shins until she was standing straight up. She repeated the process four more times while gently touching the ground. The fifth time she stood, she took a step toward the rack and set the bar on the arms.

Awesome, she thought. She added up the weight in her head

and wrote it in her notebook. A new personal record for her dead lift of 250 pounds.

Alex took a few more sips of water and then removed the weights from each side of the bar, replacing them so someone could use them. She placed her clamps back in her small sling bag and picked up her towel and water bottle. On to the bench press.

"Hey, Alex," one of the young trainers said.

She removed one of her earbuds. "Hi, David. How's it going?"

"Good. Having a good workout?" he asked.

"Yeah, I just set a new personal record for my dead lift."

"Wow. That's great. Keep at it," David said.

Alex smiled. "Looks like your client is here." She nodded at the woman she recognized as one of his regular training clients.

"See you later," he said.

Kimberly A. Biggerstaff © 2024

Alex replaced her earbud and went on with her workout. After an hour she went into the locker room to place her lifting gloves and small bag in her locker. A quick stop in the bathroom and she went upstairs for a thirty-minute run on the treadmill. She nodded and waved at one of the female trainers she knew. Wendy had trained Alex a few times over the years, and they'd become friends. Sometimes they'd go out for sushi and drinks. Alex had been coming to this gym for a couple of years. She'd seen trainers and managers come and go. Only a few had been there longer than her.

After a cooldown she went back downstairs and did some stretching and foam rolling, and then she went back to the locker room. The lockers were for use only when someone was there using the gym. If you kept a lock on a locker overnight or longer and they found out, they'd cut it off. No point in paying for a locker when she didn't need to. She placed the lock and everything in her backpack and swung it on her shoulder.

Kimberly A. Biggerstaff © 2024

On her way out to her vehicle another young man nodded and said, "Hey."

She stopped and looked at him. She looked around and walked over to him as he walked to his trunk and opened it.

"Still interested?" he asked.

"Yeah," she said.

He was nervous and looked around as he unzipped the duffel bag. He let her look inside. Lots of pill bottles, some ziplocks with syringes, and a few small bottles with clear liquid. "We said five hundred, right?" he asked in a scratchy, quiet voice.

She sighed. "Yeah." She took the backpack off her shoulder and unzipped a pocket. Reaching in, she grabbed an envelope. "Here you go. This better be good," she said, handing him the envelope.

"It's fine. I wouldn't cheat you," he said, handing her a small brown paper bag.

"Yeah, but I would. I'd also lie to you," she said as she pulled out her badge and showed it to him. Three other agents came out from behind cars and surrounded them.

"Cut!" the director on the set yelled. "That was great, Alex. Are you sure you don't want to quit your day job and go into acting?"

"No way!" she said. "You know my strength workouts are about an hour. The dead lift and then other stuff."

"Yes, I'm aware. We got some good shots of you doing the other exercises. We're going to cut the shots, edit them, and put them together so it'll look like an hour has passed. I just wanted to concentrate on that one part of the dead lift. It's a process. We shoot a lot of footage, but we cut out quite a bit. Some scenes won't even make it in the movie. Don't worry about it," the director told her.

"Are we done?"

"We're done for today. Thanks again, Alex."

She smiled. "No problem. It is a nice change of pace."

Alex Yates was an Air Force Office of Special Investigations special agent. She'd been in the air force for three years and then decided to try and become an agent. After the paperwork and interviews, she was accepted for training, and was eventually assigned to MacDill Air Force Base in Tampa, Florida. This was a reenactment of her first case as an agent. A film crew was making a movie based on that case. Alex was asked to consult, but she kept correcting the lead actress until one day the young woman finally yelled at her, "If you think you can do better, then be my guest!" and she walked off the set.

"Okay," Alex said, and she picked up the prop and continued the scene. The director was so impressed he hired her on the spot. They only had to reshoot a few scenes.

The good thing was that the movie was being shot on location right where it had happened. No traveling involved, although Alex enjoyed traveling out of town on occasion.

Kimberly A. Biggerstaff © 2024

"Alex, just a reminder that we don't need you tomorrow. You're not in any of the scenes we're shooting," the assistant director told her.

"Right. A day off," she said.

"See you the day after at five a.m."

"Ugh," she groaned. She grabbed her gear and went to her trailer.

As soon as she walked in, a man grabbed her arm and pushed her down to the floor. He held a knife to her throat.

"I've been waiting a long time for this, Agent Yates," he said, pushing the knife closer and closer until the blade began to retract back into its handle. "They don't make knives like they used to," he said, bending down and kissing her.

"I hope you knew that was a prop before you held it to my throat," Alex said.

"What's a prop?" he said, smiling his best smile. He had one of those Hollywood smiles with really straight white teeth. "Are you finished for the day?"

"Yes. Mind getting off me?"

Kimberly A. Biggerstaff © 2024

"No. I thought we'd do it right here on the floor," he said, pushing her T-shirt up slowly.

"Jack. There's a couch right there," she said, glancing to the left.

"Are you getting soft on me?"

"No. My hip hurts."

"Aww, poor baby. Let me massage it." He leaned over to kiss her again. She pulled his shirt up, but instead of pulling it all the way off she maneuvered it around his neck and pushed him back. She was now sitting over him.

"Nice move. Been practicing that?" he asked her.

She smiled and kissed him quickly. "Oh, what the hell," she said as she pulled her shirt off and began unbuttoning his pants.

"I'm not in the mood now," he said, turning his head.

"Okay." She reached for her shirt.

He pulled her back down and, while kissing her, pulled the band out of her long brown hair, letting it fall on her shoulders.

"Ms. Yates?" A young girl knocked on the door.

They froze. "Dammit," Jack said quietly.

"Be a good boy and stay," Alex whispered to him.

"Ms. Yates?"

"One minute," Alex said, standing and putting her shirt back on. She walked the short distance to the trailer door and cracked it open. "Yes?"

"Rewrites, ma'am," she said as she handed her the pages. "Do you need anything?"

"No, thanks. I'm fine," Alex said, taking the multicolored papers and smiling at her. She was about to close the door, but the girl cleared her throat. Alex knew she had more to say.

"Um, Mr. Hailey was looking for you earlier."

"Was he? Do you know what he wanted?" Alex asked innocently.

"No, ma'am. He was just watching a few of the scenes. I guess he left."

"Addison, right?"

Kimberly A. Biggerstaff © 2024

"Yes, ma'am. Addy, if you like." She grinned, impressed that the star of this movie remembered her name. The previous actress barely looked at her and ordered her around like a servant. Alex was different. Probably because she wasn't an actress.

"Addy, is Mr. Hailey a player?" Alex asked out of the blue.

"Ma'am?"

"Does he hit on all the women in his pictures?" Alex wanted to know.

"I, uh . . . it's none of my business, ma'am."

Alex could tell she was flustered. "It's okay. I know who he is. Tell him I'm not interested."

"Ma'am?"

"Never mind. I'll see you the day after tomorrow, Addy. Thanks," Alex said.

"Yes, ma'am." Addy smiled, turned on the step, and left.

Alex closed and locked the door.
Kimberly A. Biggerstaff © 2024

"Not interested?" Jack asked. He was suddenly serious, and from the floor he told her, "I'm not a player. Don't believe the rumors." He started to get up.

Alex put her foot on his chest, pushing him back down. "I said stay." She looked down at him.

He smiled. "Got your handcuffs?"

"You're not ready for that," she said, straddling him and pulling her shirt off again.

CHAPTER 2

Alex walked into her apartment and gently set her bag on the floor with one hand. Her other hand was gripping the Glock 19 on her waist. She scanned the dark room and then turned the light on. Satisfied no one was in the apartment, she turned and locked the dead bolt and then put the chain on. After letting her breath out, she went to the fridge and grabbed a beer. She checked her phone and saw the missed call. Then it barked. She had a special ringtone for her partner.

"Robby. Didn't want to come watch your partner save the world?"

"I lived the real thing. Maybe tomorrow."

"I'm off tomorrow. Next day," Alex told him.

"I still can't believe you're doing this. Or that they're letting you."

"It's good public relations," Alex said. "That's what they say anyway. You know the acting is like undercover work."

He laughed. "Yeah, you are good under the covers."

"Funny, Robby. You're a funny guy. And how would you know?"

"Nothing. I don't date my partners."

"Well, since I'm your first female partner . . . I mean it's okay if you bat for the other team," she teased him.

"You are hilarious. I'll see you the day after tomorrow. And stay away from Jack," he warned her.

"Jack who?" She hung up.

*****

Jack Hailey used to be a cop. A really good one. His father owned a production company in Florida and had been trying to make military and cop movies. He got frustrated in Hollywood with all the politics and fake people. They didn't know what

Kimberly A. Biggerstaff © 2024

the real world was like. So he picked up, went to Florida, and started his own company. His son, Jack Jr., did a stint in the Army and then joined the police force. A few years later Jack Sr. had an unexpected heart attack. After some consideration, Jack Jr. decided to take up his father's torch. When he was young he loved hanging out at the studios. He learned a lot from his father and was doing a great job running the company. It was profitable, and he loved making military and police movies. One of his movies even won an Academy Award for the lead actor.

Jack was always on the hunt for new projects. Six months ago he'd heard about Agent Yates and her case. He knew it had to be a movie. After getting permission from the Air Force, he went to meet her. He was struck. She was only five foot six but carried herself like she was eight feet tall. Brown hair pulled back in a ponytail, a black Calvin Klein suit with a light-purple Ralph Lauren oxford shirt that was perfectly starched. Her fashionable black boots were shined to a T. They were low enough that she could chase a suspect down if needed, but high enough to give her the height to look some in the eyes.

Jack asked her to be a consultant so he'd have a reason to see her. When the director told him she'd chased their star away and he hired her, Jack was even more impressed. He came to the set and watched her. One day during a break he discreetly asked her to dinner. She said no.

But Jack asked her three more times. Each time she said no, so he eventually stopped. He could take a hint. She made it obvious that she didn't want to go out with him, so he came around less often. When he did come to the set or on location, he'd leave without talking to her. But Jack's curiosity got the best of him, and he needed to know why she turned him down. So one day he asked her.

"Are you married or do you have a boyfriend?"

"No."

"So, you just don't like me?" he said, staring at her.

"I never said that."

"All you've said is no. Why?" He tried to make her laugh. "Do I smell?"

With a straight face she said, "No, you're ugly." Then she turned on a heel and walked away.

He watched her and then cracked a smile. Then he wondered if she was serious. Did she really think he was ugly? He went back to his office and stepped into the bathroom attached to his office and looked in the mirror. He may not have been the most handsome guy in the world, but he thought he was all right. He was tall at six foot three. He ran a hand through his brown hair and noticed how blue his eyes were. Then he scratched his close-cropped neatly kept beard. He smiled and looked at his teeth. Realizing what he was doing, he huffed and left the bathroom.

"She's messing with me." He never had a problem getting dates for award shows or anything. In fact, he had a bit of a reputation as a ladies man. But he wasn't. He was always a gentleman, and if he wasn't interested he'd take the woman home and leave. He did piss some women off by being too nice of a guy. They were probably the ones who'd started the rumors about him. Jack hadn't had a serious long-term relationship in a while. After three or four dates he just knew if it was worth going further.

He went home that day and called his sister. She had moved to Miami with her husband and kids.

"Hi, sis."

"What's up, little bro?"

"If I ask you question, will you give me a serious answer?"

"I'm intrigued. Go ahead."

"Am I . . . ugly?" he asked. There was silence. "Hello? Kimmi? Are you there?"

"What the hell is wrong with you?" she suddenly asked.

"What?"

Kimmi laughed. "Oh. Some girl said you were ugly and got in your head."

"Everyone knows what a great detective you are. Just answer the question," Jack said.

"Jack. She's messing with you. No, you're not ugly. Why all the . . . you really like her."

"No, I don't," he said, acting like a fifth grader who was getting teased by his buddies.

"Yes, you do," Kimmi said. "Just ask her out."

Jack sighed. "I did. Four times she shot me down."

"So this is the first time a girl's turned you down."

"No. There was a girl in high school," he said.

"One girl. All this time. One girl." She laughed at her little brother's sudden lack of confidence. "Do you need a pep talk? You're a strong, confident, handsome—"

"Goodbye, Kimmi," Jack interrupted her.

"Good luck, Jack." She hung up.

Alex is messing with me, Jack thought. He tried to get her out of his head, but he couldn't. So he came up with a plan.

The next day he showed up on set with a paper bag over his head but with the eyes cut out so he could see. He stood there and watched as they filmed a few scenes. During a break, he walked over to Alex and said, "Hi. I'm Jack and I'm ugly. Would you have dinner with me?"

"No," she said and walked away again.

He sighed in defeat, pulled the bag off his head, and walked to his car. "Great," he said, looking at the piece of paper tucked under his windshield wiper. He gave his car a quick scan, thinking someone had hit it and left a note. It was a 1974 Corvette and he loved it. He didn't see any marks, so he read the note.

Hey Ugly, meet me at Ruth's Chris Steak House at 7, tonight. Wear a suit.

Jack smiled and went home. Finally after a month of asking she decided to go out with him.

"Wear a suit. Like I don't know how to dress for a date," he said, standing in front of his closet after his shower. He had a towel wrapped around his waist. "Pick a suit. How hard is it? Man, what is wrong with you, Jack Hailey?" He picked up his phone.

"Jacky," his sister answered.

Kimberly A. Biggerstaff © 2024

"I need help. Picking out a suit."

"Since when?"

"Since now. Come on, sis. I'm putting you on video."

He pushed the button and saw his sister's face.

"Eww. She was right, you are ugly."

"Not funny."

"I've never seen you like this. You really like her."

"Just help me."

"Show me the suits."

He flipped the camera and scanned his closet.

"Wait, that dark blue one. Armani?"

"Yeah."

"That white dress shirt and a pocket square. That tie with the subtle stripes. Is that gray or white?"

"Yes."

"What?"

"It depends on the light. It goes with the suit. Thanks, sis," Jack said, satisfied.

Kimberly A. Biggerstaff © 2024

"All right. Have her back by midnight," Kimmi teased and hung up.

Jack dressed and looked at himself in the full-length mirror. "Not bad," he said. He went out to the car. "Oh, crap," he said, looking at it. He took his jacket off and laid it neatly on the passenger seat, then put the T-tops back on. He'd made the mistake of leaving the T-tops off when he went to pick up a date only once. The woman was furious when the wind messed up her hair after she'd spent so much time fixing it. There was no second date, and he learned his lesson.

He went back inside and washed his hands. "Okay, you're fine," he said as he got in the car and went to the restaurant. He made his way inside and looked for Alex. She was at the bar, so he walked over. "Hi."

"I was beginning to wonder. Is the table ready?" she said.

"What? I don't . . . you asked me. Did you make reservations?" He got nervous and sighed. "I—"

Kimberly A. Biggerstaff © 2024

"Man, you are so gullible. I thought you were a cop?" Alex said, smiling and giving him the disk that would buzz when their table was ready.

He finally took in what she was wearing. "You look really nice," he said, glancing at her crossed legs and then meeting her brown eyes. She was wearing a little black dress and black heels. Her wavy brown hair was down and flowing over her back. "Beautiful" is what he should have said. Mentally he kicked himself for not saying beautiful. What was it with this woman? She made him feel like a teenager just starting to date. He was nervous and flustered.

"Thank you. So do you," Alex said, sipping her wine.

The date was great in Jack's opinion. He couldn't tell if Alex was enjoying it or not. Finally he asked her, "Is everything okay? You don't seem like you're having a good time. Did I do something?"

"No. This is me happy," she said.

"Oh. Okay." Then he saw her smile. "Oh, got me again. Are you always like this? Messing with people?"

Kimberly A. Biggerstaff © 2024

"No, I'm sorry," Alex told him. "You have something in your teeth."

He stared at her. He pursed his lips and set his cloth napkin on the table. "I'll take care of the bill. Nice knowing you, Ms. Yates." He stood but she grabbed his hand.

"Jack. Wait. Please don't go. I'm sorry. I'll stop," Alex said with sincerity. He gave it a few seconds and sat back down. "I went too far, I'm sorry. It happens when I get . . . nervous. I mean I like to joke around but . . . I'm sorry."

"You're nervous?" he laughed. "I had to call my sister to help me pick out my suit."

Alex smiled and they laughed. The tension between them was gone.

"Where's your car?" he asked as they walked out of the restaurant.

"You don't have to walk me to my car," she said.

"Okay, bye." He started walking away.

"Hey," she called and he stopped.

He smiled to himself. Then he got serious and turned around. "Yes?"

She nodded her head toward her right and started walking. He caught up to her and offered his arm. When they arrived at her car, she opened the door and he held it for her.

"Thank you for dinner. I had a very nice time," Alex said.

"So did I. You can ask me out again. That is if you don't mind being seen with an ugly guy."

Alex laughed. "I'm sorry about that. I just didn't want to make it too easy for you."

"Great job," Jack said. "So, would you like to go out again?"

"Maybe. Can we be discreet?"

"Yeah. No problem. I hope you don't believe the rumors about me."

"I gather my own intel and make my own decisions," Alex told him.

"Glad to hear it," Jack said. "Well, I'll call you or see you on set. Thank you for asking me out." He held his hand out to shake hers.

"Yeah, right," she said, looking at his hand. She kissed him on the cheek and got in the car. He closed the door and she drove off.

"She's going to drive me crazy," he said.

*****

They had dinner a few more times, but Alex always wanted to meet him at whatever restaurant they went to. Again his investigative curiosity crept up and he had to know.

"Are you married?" he asked.

"I thought I answered that question before. No, and no boyfriend."

"Why won't you let me pick you up?"

"I like to drive," she told him.

"All right. Next time, you pick me up," he told her.

"What?"

"Here's my address." He wrote it on the back of one of his business cards and gave it to her. "I'll call you." He kissed her and went back to his car.

Alex wasn't sure what to think. They had been taking it slow, and Jack had been a perfect gentleman. She normally had chased guys off by now, especially when she said she liked to drive.

CHAPTER 3

Jack called Alex and set up another dinner. She drove to his house on Bayshore Boulevard. It was a large home overlooking the water. She parked in the circular driveway and got out and rang the bell.

"Hi. Come on in," he said. He was wearing slacks and an oxford shirt.

"Are you ready?" Alex asked.

"Almost. Follow me," he said, walking to another room.

Alex hesitated but followed him. He led her to the dining room. The table was set for two, and there were candles lit. "I thought we were going out," she said.

"I changed my mind and made dinner."

"You cooked?"

He smiled at her surprise. "Yes. When my parents divorced my sister and I came out here with my father. He hired a cook for us when he had to work late. She taught us. She made it fun. Anyway, I hope you like seafood."

"I'm allergic," she said.

He hesitated, then said, "No you're not. Our first dinner you had the sea bass."

Alex smiled at the fact that he remembered what she'd had. "No, I'm not." He pulled out her chair and she sat down.

*****

"Well, I'm impressed," Alex told him when she set her fork down. "You can cook. Probably better than me."

"How about that tour of the house?" Jack asked.

"Uh, okay," she said, standing after he came over and held her chair.

"Like I said, this was my father's house. When he died I bought my sister's half and moved in."

Kimberly A. Biggerstaff © 2024

They walked around the large home. Since the kitchen was close they saw it first. It was an open floor plan, but he told her about some of the upgrades he had made. Stainless steel appliances and a brick backsplash. He put in a gas stove, and the island was large with granite countertops. They moved on to the living room and the study. The study was more personal. He stood in the doorway and wanted to move on, but Alex went inside. She noticed the framed photo on the wall.

"Your family?" she asked.

"Yeah. My sister Kim and my father, Jack Sr. It was taken about a year before he had his heart attack."

Another photo was of Jack getting his detective's badge and there was one of his police academy graduation. She looked at the books on a shelf. "Tom Clancy, Robert Ludlum, Mark Greaney. I sense a theme here." She smiled.

"I like action, police, military, and . . . sci-fi," he said as if afraid to admit it.

"I love the classics, but a few years ago I came across a series by David Weber."

He smiled at her and went to his desk and pulled out a paperback. Holding it up for her to see the cover, he said, *"On Basilisk Station."*

Alex smiled back. "It seems we have some things in common." They looked at each other silently.

He set the book down and said, "Um, let's move on." He went to the door and she followed him out. When they arrived at the theater room, he asked if she wanted to watch a movie. "I watch the dailies in here."

"The what?"

"They send over whatever was shot for the day and I watch them. I try not to micromanage, but I like to be informed."

Alex agreed to watch a movie with him. He retrieved some snacks and drinks, and they sat in the leather stadium seating. Jack let her pick the movie.

About halfway through he made his move and held her hand. Before Alex knew it they were in his bedroom. He held her and fell asleep. Alex lay there wondering how many women had been there. This was their fifth date. She bet some of those actresses wouldn't wait that long. Then she thought, *You are so judgmental, Alex. He's a nice guy.* She closed her eyes.

*****

Jack woke up but when he looked around, Alex wasn't there. He got up and went to the bathroom. He took a quick shower and put on briefs and shorts. He looked out one of the second-story windows and saw Alex's car. "Still here." He smiled and went downstairs to the kitchen to make some coffee. He was checking his email when the door beeped indicating it opened. Alex came into the kitchen. She was in her running gear.

"Morning," he said. "Good run?"

"Yeah. I woke early and had my gear in the trunk. Nice neighborhood."

"Coffee?"

"Yes. Thanks."

"Should I ask how you got out without setting off the alarm?" he asked.

Kimberly A. Biggerstaff © 2024

"Did you set the alarm?" she asked sarcastically.

"Don't worry, I'll fix it. No damage."

He smiled as he made her a cup in the Keurig coffee maker sitting on the counter. "Take anything?"

"Sweet'N Low."

He retrieved a box from the cupboard, and she placed a packet in her mug and stirred it.

"What would you like for breakfast? I have cereal, eggs, frozen pancakes, oatmeal, breakfast burritos."

"A breakfast burrito would be fine."

"It's frozen. That okay?"

"It's fine. I have a lot of frozen meals in my freezer too," Alex said, taking the burrito and opening it. "Just need a plate to nuke it. Do you have Tabasco and salsa?"

"Uh, yeah, let me look." He looked around in the large butler's pantry for the Tabasco sauce and then pulled a jar of salsa from the refrigerator. He had a burrito too. They ate at the island in the middle of the large open kitchen.

"May I use your shower?" she asked when she was finished.

"Yeah, help yourself. Let me know if you need any items."

"I have some things. We keep an overnight bag with us when we're working." She placed her dish and mug in the dishwasher after rinsing them. She grabbed her bag that she had left by the door and went upstairs to take a shower.

When she came back she walked over and kissed him. "Thank you. I had a nice time."

"Wait. Are you leaving? I thought we could do something today," Jack said.

"I can't. I have some errands to run," Alex said.

"Oh, well. Okay." He was disappointed but understood. "I had a great time," he told her.

She smiled and walked to the back door. The garage and driveway where her car was located was at the rear of the house. They walked through the back patio to a gate. He opened it for her and walked with her to her car. She unlocked it and again he held the door for her. "I'll see you later."

"Yeah," he said and then gave her a long, soft kiss. "Bye."

"Bye," she said, sitting down and starting her car. He closed the door and she backed out and drove off.

Alex drove back to her apartment, and as she approached her door she instinctively placed a hand in her bag and gripped her weapon. The duffel bag was slung over her shoulder, and with her other hand she quietly and carefully unlocked the door. After entering and glancing around, she loosened her grip and went to her bedroom. She took her running gear out of her bag, did a load of laundry, and repacked her bag with supplies. She checked the smaller bag inside. It contained her weapon, four magazines, and badge with credentials. Satisfied, she placed it in the closet by the front door. She figured out what errands she needed to get done and made her list.

CHAPTER 4

Alex's relationship with Jack was progressing. She was very happy and so was Jack. They went out a couple more times, and Alex spent the night at Jack's both times. But again she drove herself.

*****

Present day . . . the day after they made love in her trailer.

"Hi, partner," Alex said, walking up behind Robby.

"Hi," he said between bites of a donut. "I don't know how you're going to keep your figure with all that food over there."

"A lot of running and extracurricular activities."

"Dammit, Alex," he whispered to her. "I thought I told you to stay away from him."

"Are you jealous or just looking out for me?"

"I'm not jealous. I don't date my partners. Even one as hot as you," he teased her.

"Don't worry. I'm just having fun," Alex said. "Come on. Let's go to my trailer. I need to get you away from those donuts."

Alex and Robby went to her trailer. Robby noticed as she took a breath and slowly opened the door. She carefully went inside and saw a vase of flowers.

"Uh-oh," Robby said, looking around to make sure he wasn't there. "You might be having fun, but I think he's hooked."

Alex smiled, taking the card and reading it. There wasn't anything to read. Just a smiley face. But it was signed – *Ugly.*

A knock at the door wiped the smile from her face. She answered it. "Hello, Mr. Hailey."

"I was just checking that . . ."

Robby peeked over her shoulder so he could see him. "Hi, Mr. Hailey."

"Robby. Nice to see you. And I told you to call me Jack."

Robby smiled. "Jack. I hope it's okay that I came to visit."

Alex stepped aside and let Jack in. "Of course. You are welcome anytime. It's your movie too. Nice flowers to bring to your partner."

"I'd never give her flowers. Well, unless she was in the hospital."

"Aww. What a guy," Alex teased Robby. He was about eight years older than her. She had been partnered with him right after she finished her specialized training, and they got along great. Robby was like an older brother, but she was learning a lot from him.

"Well, I wanted to make sure everything was going okay on set. Any issues or problems?"

"No. Everything's fine."

Kimberly A. Biggerstaff © 2024

"Okay, good. See you later," Jack said, leaving.

"Later, Ugly," Robby said.

Jack paused for a second and then left.

Robby laughed after he left. "So what's the deal?"

"He asked me out four times and I said no. He wanted to know why I turned him down and asked if he smelled. I told him that he was ugly."

Robby laughed some more and sat on the couch. "You're bad, Alex. He's probably got a complex now."

"He's fine. And he's a gentleman."

"How many times have you gone out?"

"I don't know, five or six?" Alex said, getting a bottle of water from the fridge. "Want one?"

"Sure." He continued, "Wow. Longest yet. Has he asked why you have to drive?"

"Yes. Well, he asked why I meet him. I told him I like to drive," Alex said.

"Well, if he's still around in a month maybe he's okay," Robby said. "I want to watch the guy playing me shoot his scene. See you later." He winced a little when he stood.

"Still hurt?"

"Sometimes. It's probably going to rain." Robby smiled and walked to the door. "You know, maybe you should talk to someone about entering places," he said, stopping and looking at her.

"I'm a cop. I'm cautious. You don't check for exits and sit against walls?"

"Point taken. I'm just . . . concerned, Alex," he said, slightly smiling at her.

"Later, partner," Alex said.

"Later, Gator," Robby said, pulling the door behind him.

"Ms. Yates. They're ready for you in makeup," Addy said just before Robby shut the door.

"On my way," Alex said.

*****

Kimberly A. Biggerstaff © 2024

Alex was lying on the couch in her trailer after a long day. Her eyes were closed, but she had a beer in her hand set on her stomach. She startled herself awake and almost spilled the beer. "I need to go home," she said to herself. She finished the beer and grabbed her bag. It was late. She walked to her car and got in. There was a note on the windshield. She unrolled her window and reached for it.

Text me when you get home. Ugly.

Alex thought about it and texted right away. Leaving lot now. I have a late call tomorrow if you'd like to come over. It was the first time she'd invited him over to her apartment. She preferred his place. But who wouldn't?

Now?

If you like. Text me and I'll let you in or wait for me at the gate. Alex's apartment complex had a gate with codes. She changed her codes all the time, but it still wouldn't be difficult to get in. You could walk in through the pedestrian gate.

Jack jumped at the chance to go to her place. He gathered some clothes and toiletries and placed them in a backpack and ran down to his car. He had already placed her address in his phone. He pulled up the directions on the app and made his way to her.

Instead of texting he called. "I'm at the gate."

"It's 27538 and pound," Alex said quickly and then disconnected the call.

"Shit . . . 27538 oh and pound," he said, pressing the buttons. She said the code so fast he wasn't sure he got it right. He looked for her building and found a spot to park a couple of cars down from hers. He had driven his truck this time. The truck came in handy at times for taking things to the lot or on location. He grabbed his backpack and swung it on his shoulder and went up the stairs to the third level. He found her apartment and knocked.

After checking the peephole she opened the door. "You certainly took your time," she said sarcastically.

"I got a speeding ticket," he said. "Can you fix it?" he joked.

"No." She was already wearing her sleep shorts and shirt for bed.

He smiled. "Do I get a tour?" he asked her.

"This is the living area, kitchen, dining table, hallway," she said, standing in place and pointing.

"You make a terrible tour guide," he said, setting his backpack on the floor by the couch. "It's a good thing you're pretty."

Alex ignored the comment. "Beer?" she asked and then she yawned.

"Yes, please." He followed her to the kitchen. "Or we can just go to bed," he said, smiling and placing his hands on her waist.

"Here's your beer," she said, holding it up.

"Are you sure you want me here?" he asked. He was getting the feeling she had changed her mind or something.

"I wouldn't have invited you if I didn't."

Kimberly A. Biggerstaff © 2024

"Rough day at work?"

"Long day. Memories," she said, looking down as she took a step back from him.

"Oh. I don't always know what they shoot. Was it when Robby got hurt?" He opened the beer.

"Yeah," she said.

"I'm sorry." He went to hug her, but she pulled away.

"I don't need a hug," she told him.

He sighed. "Maybe I should go."

"No. I don't want you to leave."

"What do you want?"

"I don't know. Company? Just someone here."

The way she said it made him feel like she just wanted anyone to be there. But he wanted to be her boyfriend. Someone she could talk to and hold when she had a bad day. A shoulder to cry on if she needed. But that wasn't what she wanted. He went to get his bag. "Get a dog," he said and left.

"Shit. Way to go Alex. You chased another one away," she said to herself. "Maybe I should get a dog." She went to the door and locked it and put the chain on. Then she went to bed.

But now she couldn't sleep. She tossed and turned. She looked at her phone and texted Robby. I chased him away.

Her phone rang. "What happened?"

"Just me being me."

"I want details," he said.

"Why are you awake?" she asked. When she texted she didn't think he'd still be up.

"I thought we were talking about you."

"The scenes today. Some of them were rough to shoot," she said. "It must have been even harder for you. I'm sorry, Robby."

"I'm dealing with it," he said, looking back at the woman rubbing his shoulders. "Ow."

"Are you having sex?"

Kimberly A. Biggerstaff © 2024

"I can multitask." He smiled. "Tell me what you said to him."

"I told him it was a rough day and he went to hug me. I told him I didn't need a hug."

"And."

"I said I just wanted company. Someone there. Then he told me to get a dog and he left."

"Alex."

"I know. I'm an idiot," she said, staring at the ceiling watching the ceiling fan go around.

"Do you like this guy or are you still just having fun?" Robby asked. "Oh my God, that feels so good."

"Seriously?"

"I'm getting a massage. Honest," he said. "Answer the question."

"I think I really like him," she admitted.

"Then apologize."

"Yeah, I know," she said. "Thanks, Robby. You're a good partner. Enjoy the sex with your escort," she said, disconnecting the call.

*****

Alex showed up the next day on set with a shepherd mix on a leash. She walked by Jack, who was talking to the director. "You can bite him," she said to the dog. He whined. She went to her trailer and a few minutes later Addy told her it was time for makeup. She brought the dog with her. "Sit. Good boy."

"What's his name, Ms. Yates?" someone asked.

"Brutto. It's Italian for Ugly. He reminds me of someone." She said it loud enough that Jack heard her.

"Awww. He's so cute. Is he trained?" Addy asked, scratching the dog behind the ears.

"A little. I need to find someone. He's potty trained and can sit. Addy, can you watch him while I shoot my scenes?"

"Yes, ma'am. You do remember I'm your personal assistant? You just never give me anything to do."

"Oh yeah. Would you find a trainer for me?"
Kimberly A. Biggerstaff © 2024

"Yes, ma'am. I'd love to. Do you want basic obedience training?"

"Yes. On and off leash. Maybe an attack command."

"Attack? Really?"

"No. Just the other stuff." She looked at the pup. "Good boy, Brutto." He barked.

*****

"You got a dog. I thought you were going to apologize," Robby said.

"I changed my mind," Alex said.

"You know dogs are a big responsibility. You have to feed it, water it, walk it, pick up after it. Can you have one in your apartment?" he asked her as they sat in her trailer.

"Yes. I checked. I just had to shell out more money towards my security deposit."

"A cat might have suited you better. They're less needy. Independent and stuck up," he teased her.

"Hey, don't you have to go to work?" she reminded him as she ignored his comment.

"Desk duty sucks," he said, petting the dog who was in his lap. "When are you finished with this movie?"

"I don't know. We have to be close," she said.

"Well, hurry up. I want to get back out there with you."

"Aww, you miss me."

"Yes, I do."

"How was your . . . massage?"

"Wonderful. You should have come over and gotten one."

"You really did get a massage?"

"Yeah. In between the sex." He smiled at her. "Okay, I'm going. Paperwork waits for no man." He moved Brutto, who had fallen asleep. The dog got up and went to the door. "Brutto needs out," he told her.

"Okay." She picked his leash up and took him out. She walked over to a grassy area and let him pee and sniff awhile. "Good boy. Let's go."

"Ms. Yates, I can take Brutto now. I found a great place," Addy said.

"Oh, okay." She bent down to Brutto. "Be a good boy at school. Don't let the other dogs pick on you." She rubbed his head and kissed him between his ears. "Thanks, Addy."

"You're welcome. Makeup is ready for you in ten minutes," she told her, taking Brutto's leash.

Alex walked over to the director. "I was curious. How much longer do we have on this picture?"

"If things go well, another three months or so of shooting. Is there a problem?" he asked, suddenly worried.

"No, just curious. Shooting out of order made me lose track of where we are." Alex walked over to makeup and sat in the chair.

CHAPTER 5

The next three months were miserable for Alex. The only thing she enjoyed was Brutto. Alex didn't realize how much she missed Jack. He only came to the lot a few times and stayed away

 from her.

Jack was also having a hard time. He had fallen quickly for Alex and was hoping to get to know her better. He found her interesting and intriguing, but he had stayed away from her.

One day on set Jack came up to the director and asked if they were shooting the car scene.

"Yeah, it's just a simple scene with conversation," he confirmed.

"I want to make a minor change. Just try it. Probably won't work." Jack then whispered in his ear.

"Okay, listen up," the director yelled. He got up and went closer to the actors and car. "Alex, I'd like to try you in the passenger seat."

"Uh, no," she told him.

"Would you just try? We want to see if it makes a difference."

"That's not the way it was," Alex said.

"I realize that, but we—"

"Fine!" she yelled. She walked over to the passenger side. She felt her heart rate increase. Her breathing increased as she touched the door handle and opened the door. Her hand started shaking as she looked at the seat. She slammed the door and walked over to Jack. "Bastard!" she yelled and punched him across the jaw. Alex was quick and he was willing to take a slap. But the punch caught him off guard. She went back to her trailer.

Kimberly A. Biggerstaff © 2024

Ron stared at Jack as the assistant director, Rose said, "Mr. Hailey! Are you okay?"

"Yeah. Change it back, Ron," he said, holding his jaw and going back to his office.

*****

Once again Jack kept his distance. If they needed him he'd be there. On the final day of the shoot he needed to be there.

He stayed out of the way and only talked to people who talked to him. That evening the director yelled, "Cut! Well, ladies and gentlemen, that is a wrap! Well done, everyone!" They all clapped, cheered, shook hands, and hugged each other.

After all the festivities were over, Alex went to her trailer. Robby was inside waiting for her with Brutto. The dog bounded over and sat in front of her. "Speak," Alex said.

"*Woof.*"

"Lay down."

The dog complied.

"Roll over."

Kimberly A. Biggerstaff © 2024

"Good boy!" Alex looked around and gave him a treat. Then she rubbed his belly. "Well, it's over, Robby."

Robby looked at her. "Yep. Are you going to be a downer at work?"

"What are you talking about?"

"You've been mopey. Just go apologize."

"No. It's too late. I'll get over it. Once we're back at work I'll forget all about him." She forced a smiled.

Robby had his doubts. "Yeah. Sure."

*****

Two months later.

"Jack, you need to get over here," the director said on the phone.

"What's going on?"

"There's been an . . . accident on set. One of the extras is dead."

"Lock everything and everyone down. Don't touch anything. No one leaves. I'm on my way," Jack said. He ran outside to the golf cart and drove over to the soundstage. The studio was in an old warehouse building that Jack's father had got a deal on in Tampa. Eventually he purchased some nearby office buildings, and Jack Jr. had expanded even more when the studio was doing really well.

"Did you call the police?" Jack asked the director.

"Yes. Jack, he was an extra working part-time." The director paused and then told him the next part. "He's an airman from the base."

"Oh. You're sure?" Jack asked.

"Positive."

"They need to be informed. Here, call this number," Jack said, holding his phone to show the director a phone number. "She'll know what to do. I need to call our attorneys. What the hell happened?"

"Prop gun malfunctioned. Rifle, whatever," he said. "It's still unclear."

"Shit."

The police arrived and got started on their investigation. The director made the call that Jack couldn't.

Kimberly A. Biggerstaff © 2024

"Yates," Alex said.

"Alex, this is Ron Ford from the studio."

"Yes, don't tell me we have to reshoot something?" she said.

"No. There's been a death on set. He's one of yours."

Alex straightened in her chair and gave him her full attention. "What do you mean?" she asked.

"He's an airman from MacDill working as an extra for us."

She let out a breath and asked, "Okay. Did you call the police?"

"Yeah, they just arrived," Ron told her.

"Okay, I'll brief my boss and someone will be over," Alex said. "Thanks for the heads-up." She hung up and went to her boss.

"Ma'am?" Alex said, knocking on her commanding officer's door.

"Yates, come in," the CO said.

"I was just informed that one of our airmen died at Hailey's Comet Studios."

The lieutenant colonel set her pen down and sighed. "You're sure? How do you know?"

"The director I worked for called me."

"All right. You and Robertson go."

"Ma'am, I—"

"You know the people and the area. You got the call. Go."

"Yes, ma'am," Alex said, turning around and leaving the office. Alex was hoping she'd give the case to another team. But if it were her, she'd have done the same thing. Alex knew them just enough to gain their trust. She wasn't even sure who else was there on the set. Ford might be the only one.

"Come on, Robby, we got a case," she said to her partner.

"Great! Well, you know what I mean." Robby was excited to get off desk duty and get back in the field.

Kimberly A. Biggerstaff © 2024

"Glad you're happy," she said, picking up her bag and the keys to their car.

"Any chance I can—"

"No," Alex said, knowing he was going to ask to drive.

Before they left the office their boss called from her doorway. "Yates."

"Yes, ma'am," Alex said, walking over to her.

"Anything I need to know? Possible conflicts of interest?" she asked.

"No, ma'am." Alex began to turn but stopped. "Ma'am, I, uh . . . the owner . . . Mr. Hailey. Well . . . we, uh . . ."

"Are you currently involved with anyone at that studio?" her boss asked. She couldn't let Alex stand there struggling to tell her.

"No, ma'am. Not since about three months before we finished the movie."

"Fine. Take off."

Alex briefed Robby on the way to the studio. She pulled up to the gate.

Kimberly A. Biggerstaff © 2024

"Hello, Ms. Yates. They're waiting for you inside Soundstage 1," the security guard said. He was told to expect her or someone from the Air Force. He was glad it was her.

"Thank you." Alex smiled at him and drove on.

"You going to be okay?" Robby asked.

"It's our job. I'll be fine," Alex said.

"Oh, before we go in, one joke. So, we've got a Brandon Lee situation?" Robby said.

"Who?"

"Brandon Lee. He was shot on the movie set of *The Crow.* You know, Bruce Lee's son." He glanced over at her and saw the big smile on her face. "How long were you going to let me keep talking?"

"I was hoping you'd recap the entire movie for me. It's been a while since I saw it. Recap that case. What happened?"

"Squib load. Something was jammed in the barrel from the day before, and then the weapon wasn't properly checked the next day. When it was fired there was enough force to dislodge what was in the barrel, and it hit Lee in the abdomen, killing him."

"The armorer on my set was really good. I don't think he'd make that mistake. But we'll talk to whoever the armorer was."

Robby's phone chimed and he read the text. He smiled at Alex and said, "The boss said to give you the reigns. Congrats."

"What?"

"You're the lead agent. My little sis is growing up." He playfully punched her in the arm.

Alex had mixed feelings about that. She was glad her CO had confidence in her, but she was a little uncomfortable because she knew these people. She parked the car near the soundstage, and Alex took a deep breath. "Okay. Let's go, Agent Robertson."

"Yes, ma'am, Agent Yates."

They went inside and showed their credentials to a police officer standing guard. Alex saw the director, Ron Ford, and walked over to him.

"Mr. Ford," Alex said in a professional manner.

"Ms. Yates."

"Uh, Agent Yates and Agent Robertson, please," Alex said, emphasizing the word "agent."

"Yes, of course. Sorry."

"I know you probably told the police what happened, but could you tell us, please."

Alex and Robby listened and took notes. They asked a few questions and then asked to go see the body.

"He's over there. We didn't touch anything except to see if we could help him."

Alex and Robby put the crime-scene booties over their shoes and went over to the body. Alex introduced herself and Robby to the local police and the detectives standing nearby.

"Detective Vickers. Here's his ID card, Agent." The detective handed her a bag with the victim's wallet and military ID showing. "He's yours. Care to join us?"

"A joint investigation? Sure," Alex said.

"We're a little shorthanded and overwhelmed, so we'd appreciate the help. I was told you're familiar with the area and staff?"

"Yeah, I was helping out with a movie. We finished a couple of months ago."

"She was the star of the movie. Based on one of our cases," Robby told him.

Alex didn't appreciate him calling her the star and gave him a look.

"Was that a joint DEA case a couple of years ago?" Vickers asked.

"Yes. And I'm not the star," Alex said. "What can we do to help, Detective Vickers?"

"What are your initial thoughts?" He wanted to feel them out and see what this young agent thought.

Kimberly A. Biggerstaff © 2024

"An accident. But we need to check the prop and talk to the armorer."

"Good. Would you come with me? He's over there," Vickers told her.

"Robby, why don't you speak to the owner?" Alex asked him. She didn't even say his name.

"Mr. Hailey?" he asked, knowing who she meant.

She just looked at him and went with Vickers. Robby asked around and found Jack. He walked over to him just as he finished a phone call.

"Mr. Hailey. I'm Agent Robertson. I need to ask you some questions." Robby could also be professional.

Jack understood the formality and replied, "Agent. I was in my office when my director, Mr. Ford, called me." Jack told him everything he knew and did. Having been a cop he knew the drill and was prepared.

"A little different being on the other side?" Robby asked when he finished.

"Yes. Anything you need, let me know." Jack looked around every once in a while.

Robby noticed. "She's with the local detective, Vickers. It's their case, but he asked for assistance."

"She who? Are we done?" Jack asked.

"Yes, sir. I'll be in touch if there's anything else," Robby said. Obviously Alex and Jack had unresolved issues concerning their relationship. "This is going to be fun," Robby said to himself after Jack walked away.

CHAPTER 6

Vickers and Alex went to talk to the armorer. "I'm Detective Vickers with Tampa PD, and this is Agent Yates with Air Force OSI."

"I know Agent Yates. Ma'am," Carl said.

"It's okay, just relax. We need to ask some questions," Alex said, trying to calm the visibly upset man. He nodded.

All the weapons were kept locked in a safe in another room that was also secured. "Look, my staff and I are very careful. Ever since that incident on the set of *The Crow* I don't take any chances."

"Vickers, Yates, I need to talk to you," Robby said appearing in the doorway of the armory.

"What is it, Robby?" Alex asked as they walked over to him.

"The medical examiner arrived. I was looking at the entrance and exit wound. It was at an angle that rules out the suspect. There's no way Trevino, the actor, could have killed him. And we found the round—5.56."

"Dammit. Let's go see," Vickers said. They went back to the scene and looked.

"Go ahead, Robby," Alex said.

"Airman Collins was standing here and Trevino was over there with his prop gun. Based on Collins's height, where he was standing, and the angle of the wound . . ." He paused to step in place, took a laser and placed it on his chest at the height of the entrance wound. Robby pointed the laser at the approximate angle the path of the bullet supposedly traveled. "The exit wound makes this the path of the bullet. I think the shot came from up there." They all followed the path of the red laser with their eyes.

"Let's go have a look," Vickers said. They walked to some stairs and up on a catwalk to find the area where a possible shooter could have been. Vickers was leading the way.

"Fuck me," Vickers said, stopping. "Yates."

Alex looked at the area but was quiet.

"Goddamn it," Robby said.

It was like a small shrine. There was an unlit candle, three different photos of Alex when she was on set, and a single 5.56mm shell casing standing next to a 5.56 round. Underneath the shell casing and round was a yellow Post-it note. On the note was written a set of four numbers and then "10-24."

"What are those first set of numbers?" Vickers asked.

Alex swallowed. "My badge number."

"That's a threat, Alex. You're off the case," Robby said.

The next set of numbers was a local code the police used. "10-24 is our code for officer down. I agree. You need to go back to your base," Vickers said. "Take her back, Robertson. Wait. Any idea who this might be?"

Alex glanced at Robby and then back at Vickers. "Yeah. The Sea Cow Gang," Alex said.

"How do you know?"

"Look." She pointed to a steel bar on the catwalk with a sticker of a manatee on it and the letters SCG.

"Son of a bitch," Robby said. "Let's go, Alex. I'll be back, Vickers."

"What? No, I'm not leaving," Alex said with conviction. No way was she going to let this gang kick her off the case. She'd taken these guys down once and could do it again.

"They did this to draw you out," Robby said.

"They could have taken me anytime. Something else is going on," Alex said.

"Get out of here, Yates. Now," Vickers told her.

Alex begged to stay and help. "I can help. I know them, I dismantled them."

Kimberly A. Biggerstaff © 2024

"We will need your help," Vickers said. "But I need you safe for now. Go back to base. At least for now."

"Alex, please," Robby said. "I'll keep you informed."

Alex had another good look around for any clues. "Okay."

Robby went with her back downstairs. Vickers radioed for a forensics team to come up to the shrine.

"That kid was collateral damage. He was an innocent used to get my attention," Alex said.

"Yeah, probably," Robby agreed. "But why don't you go back to base and run background on him. That's how you can help. Make sure he's not connected to the Sea Cows. Stupid name. I like the Manatees."

"You said that when we first found out about them," Alex reminded him.

"Still true. I'll send a couple of officers with you and stay here. You go back and brief the boss and get started on that background."

Jack was milling about nearby, and he glanced at Robby and Alex.

"Officers, you two, come here," Robby called out.

"I have to drive," Alex said.

"I know. Take the car. I'll find a way back," he told her. He asked the two officers to escort her back to the base. "She'll drive, okay?"

One of the officers said, "If she's in danger, shouldn't we—"

"It has to be this way or you let her drive your car," Robby told them.

"Okay, sir. Jones, you follow so we have a way back. I'll ride with her. Will that be okay?" the officer asked Robby.

"Yeah, thanks. I'll tell Vickers what you're doing," Robby said. Then he walked them all out. "Be safe, Alex. Don't do anything stupid, please."

Alex smiled at him. "I'll go straight to base and get started on the background check of Collins."

"I'll call the boss and check on you," Robby warned.

Alex sighed and drove off with one officer getting in the passenger seat of her government car. The cruiser followed.

Jack had been watching. Robby went over to him and they walked back inside. "If you hadn't been a cop I'd ignore you. But I think you need to see this."

"See what?" Jack asked.

"This wasn't an accident," Robby said, leading him up to the catwalk.

"What the hell, Robertson?" Vickers said.

"He was a cop. One of you. He might know something," Robby told him.

Jack looked around at the shrine. He bent down to get a closer look but didn't touch anything. He was suddenly very concerned. "Shit. You sent her back to base?" Jack asked.

"Yeah. She's going to run background on our airman. I had to give her something to do or she'd be in our shit. I sent two of your officers with her, Vickers."

The detective groaned and said, "Yeah, okay."

"Those photos were taken on set," Jack told them.

One of the forensic techs handed him a photo. "Uh, sir. This was found under the Post-it."

"Oh, uh, Mr. Hailey." Vickers showed him the photo, but Jack didn't touch it. He didn't have gloves on. It was a photo of Alex and Jack on the floor of her trailer. She had her shirt off and he was about to kiss her.

Jack's face got hard. Now he was really pissed. Someone watched them as they made love in her trailer.

"You know she named the dog Ugly," Robby said, trying to distract him.

"What?"

"His name is Brutto; that's b-r-u-t-t-o. Brutto is Italian for ugly," he told him. "I told her to apologize."

Vickers had to ask. "Are you guys still . . . involved?"

"No. Not for about five months?" He wasn't sure of the timeline.

Robby knew and confirmed it. "Yes. Three months on set and two more of putting up with her miserable ass back at her real job. Is her ass as nice as her breasts?" he said, stretching to look at the photo again, but Vickers told the tech to bag it for evidence.

"Shut up," Jack said angrily to Robby.

"She's my partner. I'm kidding," Robby told them. "I've seen her ass, and she saw my dick hanging out when those bastards shot me in the hip. I'll be damned if I'll let anyone hurt her. She's like a little sister to me." He turned and walked away.

"The Sea Cows?" Jack asked Vickers. Jack had a feeling that was who might want revenge.

The detective pointed to the sticker. "Yeah."

Jack told Vickers what happened. "They were distributing drugs on base. Alex played a strung-out spouse and made contact. They were following a suspect when someone made them. Firefight. Robby took a round in the hip. Alex got him to safety and went after the shooter. They fought and she killed him. He was the leader's little brother. Only sixteen."

"Sounds like a good movie."

"Yeah, that's the plan. You've got other photos, Vickers. Do you need that one?" Jack said hopefully.

"What do you think?"

"Yeah, I know. Does she know about that one?"

"No. She left before the tech boys found it," Vickers said.

"Ford can show you her old trailer, but there's another actor in there now. Maybe you can still find something. Let me know if I can be of help," Jack said, starting to leave.

"Yeah," Vickers said and let him go.

Jack stopped and turned around. "Before you ask, I was in my office when the kid was shot. There was no way I could shoot him from up there and get back to my office before Ford called me. He called on the landline. No cell phones during the scenes."

"Thanks," Vickers said, writing in his notebook.

Jack went back to his office and opened his mini fridge. He pulled out a beer and opened it. It took three big gulps and he finished it. He sat down on his couch and called an old friend. After the call he looked at his watch. It was getting late, and he called Robby.

"I hired protection for her," Jack said. "An old friend of mine went into the protection business."

"She's going to be pissed, but I'll thank you."

"What about you? Are you in any danger?" Jack asked him. "Forget it—you'll have protection too."

"No, I don't . . . well, I am her partner and I was there. I'm not going to be stupid. Thanks."

"Where is she?" Jack asked.

"The boss is about to send us home. I'll make sure she gets home okay."

"The guys will probably pick you up and follow from the gate. Don't freak out."

"How will I know it's them and not the bad guys," Robby asked.

"The license plates all have the letters RPS in them. Renegade Protection Services," Jack told him. "And any numbers are sequential. Like RPS456."

Kimberly A. Biggerstaff © 2024

"Thanks, Jack."

"I still care about her," Jack said. He felt like he needed to say it.

"She hasn't dated anyone longer than you. Tends to chase them away. I thought you might be different."

Jack was quiet.

"Well, I better go," Robby said. "She's giving me the evil eye from across the room."

"Stay safe," Jack told him and hung up. He sat there for a while and then gathered his things. Jack went to his car and took a drive along Bayshore Boulevard looking at the water. Eventually he made a decision and turned. He parked in a visitors parking spot and walked to Alex's apartment. He passed a man he was sure was one of the protection guys. He stopped him.

"I'm Jack Hailey. Are you with RPC?" Jack said, testing him.

"RPS? Yes, sir. I know who you are. She's inside, and she is very mad."

Kimberly A. Biggerstaff © 2024

"Yeah, I figured. She'll probably kick me in the balls if she doesn't hit me in the face," Jack said. Then he thought, *Just swallow your pride and knock.* He took a deep breath and knocked.

*****

Alex was drinking a beer. She was pissed. She'd already guzzled the first one and was on her second. Brutto was watching her. "You'd protect me, wouldn't you?" she said to him. He cocked his head and whined. She went to his treat jar and gave him one. Then she went to get his toy. Alex threw it and he chased it. Suddenly the dog stopped and looked at the door. He ran over to it and growled. Then came the knock. He barked once and kept growling. Alex went to the door feeling for her weapon on her hip and looked through the peephole.

She tried to think of a smart-ass remark but drew a blank. So she opened the door.

"I'd like to talk to you," Jack said.

Alex thought a minute and then let him in. "Brutto, ankle." The dog leaped at his ankle and nipped it.

Kimberly A. Biggerstaff © 2024

"Ow! What the hell?" Jack said.

"Out. Good boy." She tossed Brutto a treat. "I've been waiting to try that on someone."

"Alex, I'm sorry. I'm sorry I walked away. I'm sorry I told you to get a dog. I'm sorry these guys are after you. I'm not sorry I hired the protection for you and Robby."

"Robby has protection too?"

"Yeah. He's your partner and was there. I saw the shrine."

"Big deal," Alex said, standing with her arms crossed.

Jack noticed the weapon still on her hip. "Robby tell you about the photo they found after you left?" he asked, still standing near the door.

"No, what photo?"

"You and me in the trailer . . . on the floor . . . in a compromising position." He looked away.

Alex walked to the kitchen table and picked up the beer and finished it. She went to the fridge and came back with two and handed him one.

"Thank you," Jack said, taking the beer.

Alex sat on the couch and Brutto looked at her. She patted the spot beside her, and he jumped up and put his head in her lap.

"May I sit there, or is he going to bite me?" he asked, carefully eyeing the dog.

"Go ahead," Alex said.

Jack walked over and sat down on the couch, leaving a space between him and Brutto. "You named him Ugly."

"Do you know Italian?"

"No. Robby told me."

"You said get a dog so I did."

"Where did you get him?" Jack asked, still watching the dog.

"The pound."

"Good. Plenty of lost pups need good homes," he said. "Can I pet him?"

"Yeah," she said as she scratched his ears.

Kimberly A. Biggerstaff © 2024

Jack gently petted him on the back. "He's cute." Jack smiled. "I'm sorry, Alex. I've missed you."

"I missed you too. I'm sorry. I tend to say the wrong things with guys I date and then they leave. Most leave when I won't get in the passenger seat."

"I'm sorry what I did on set that day. I had to know. Nice punch, by the way."

"I'm not telling you about that. Not now."

"It's okay. Did you find out anything about the kid? Any connections?"

"Not yet."

Jack stood up. "Let's go for a drive." He held out the keys to his Corvette. "You can drive a stick, can't you?"

"Yes."

"How many drinks have you had?" Jack asked.

"This is number three. Maybe we can wait half an hour?"

"Okay. Thank you for being responsible with my car."

He sat back down. "What do you want to do while we wait?"
Kimberly A. Biggerstaff © 2024

They looked at each other and leaned close but Brutto sat up between them and softly growled.

"Down, boy. Go play." She threw a toy that was nearby, and Brutto chased after it. Alex slid over toward Jack and they kissed.

*****

"What does this mean for us?" Alex asked.

"I missed you, Alex. I want to be with you," Jack said, holding her. "I guess it's up to you. And Brutto." He smiled as he stroked her bare arm. "Hey, has Robby seen your ass?"

"What? What kind of question is that?"

"After they found the photo, he said he's seen your ass and you saw his dick when he got shot."

She turned on her stomach and said, "I saw his Homer Simpson boxer shorts. See this scar?" She felt a small scar on the back of her leg. It was a four-inch horizontal scar three inches below her ass. "That's all he saw."

"How'd you get that?" he said, moving his hand from the scar to her ass. He left his hand there.

Kimberly A. Biggerstaff © 2024

"Maybe I'll tell you some day. Not now. Can we go for that drive now?"

"You still want to? It's late," he said.

"Yes. Can we take Brutto?" Alex asked. The dog looked at her from the floor.

"Uh, I guess we can put a towel down in the back."

Alex sat up and looked for her shirt and bra. She dressed as Jack watched her. "Come on, let's go," she said, picking the keys up.

Jack began dressing. "Bring your go bag," he said, zipping his pants.

"Why?"

"You may need a change of clothes," he told her. "If you want to stay. Totally up to you."

"Mysterious. Okay. I still get to drive?"

"Yes." He gave her a kiss.

"And Brutto can come?"

"Yes."

Alex packed a toy and some food for Brutto, grabbed her bag, and they went to his car. After getting Brutto settled in the small back area of the Corvette, Alex climbed in the driver's seat.

"You're the first person I've let drive her," Jack said.

"I'll be careful."

"Do you want the tops on?"

"No. It's a nice night," Alex said, smiling.

The protection guys were in an SUV and followed them as Jack gave her directions. Traffic was light, and it took less than forty minutes to arrive at Jack's Madeira Beach condominium. They pulled into the drive, and Alex looked at the condo.

"Is this yours?"

"My sister and I share it. She lives in Miami with her husband and kids."

"Uncle Jack?" Alex teased him.

"Yeah. She has a boy, two years old, and a girl, five."

Jack retrieved their bags, and Alex let Brutto out. The dog

found a bush to pee on and sniffed around. Jack waited and Alex called Brutto who ran up beside her.

"He's well trained," Jack said.

"Addy found a place for me. They did a great job. I had to go a few times to learn what they taught him, and they made sure he'd listen to me. They actually gave me homework. Things to work on with him."

"I hope he likes the beach," Jack said as they went up to the condo. He unlocked the door and they went inside.

"Wow, this is nice. Very modern," Alex said as she looked around.

"My father bought it during construction. He passed away before it was done. My sister and I decided to keep it."

"Great view," Alex said, opening the sliding glass door and going out on the large patio area.

"You should see the sunrise," Jack said, putting an arm around her waist as they looked out to the ocean.

"Maybe later," Alex said, turning and kissing him.

CHAPTER 7

Alex woke to the smell of bacon and coffee. Putting on a robe, she padded out to the kitchen area. Jack was cooking eggs, bacon, and hash browns. She came up behind him, wrapping her arms around his waist.

"Good morning," he said. "We were wondering if you'd ever get up." Brutto was sitting nearby, patiently waiting for scraps or anything dropped on the floor.

"Are you bribing my dog?" she asked. Alex kissed Jack on the cheek and grabbed a piece of bacon for herself.

"Yes." Jack tossed a small piece of bacon to Brutto, who caught it. "Just a little."

"We missed the sunrise," Alex said, helping herself to some coffee.

Jack smiled. "You probably needed the sleep. We were up late."

Alex heard her phone ring and sighed. She answered it. "Hello?"

"Good morning. How are you doing?" Robby asked.

"Fine. How are you?" Alex answered as she smiled at Jack.

"Fine. Any updates or problems?"

"No, nothing yet. How about on your end?"

"No, I'm going to check in with Vickers later and see what he has. Are you at home?" Robby asked.

"No. Madeira Beach."

"Are you alone? I thought I heard whispering."

"No, Brutto's here."

"Any humans?" he asked.

Alex walked into the living room and stood in front of the balcony doors. "Maybe."

Robby let out a little laugh. "Good for you. If you're happy, then I'm happy. Oooh, yeah, right there."

Kimberly A. Biggerstaff © 2024

"Oh my God, Robby. Why do you always call me when you're having sex?"

"My hip hurts from all the walking and going up and down stairs."

"Sex will not help your hip."

"I get massages too," he said as the woman smiled at him.

"Do you use the same woman all the time?"

"I . . . need . . . to go. Say hello to Jack for me," Robby said, hanging up.

Alex chuckled and went to sit at the island bar. Jack brought her a plate of scrambled eggs with cheese mixed in, bacon, and hash browns.

"Thank you."

"You've got an interesting partner there. Was he really having sex?"

"Sex and massages. He thinks it bothers me, but I think it's funny."

They had their breakfast and then went for a walk on the beach with Brutto.

*****

It was a wonderful weekend for Alex. She went back to work on Monday with her security entourage following close. She had thought about it, and since the Sea Cows had a presence on the base, she arranged for her protection to be able to follow her anywhere she went.

"You signed your guys on base?" Robby asked when he saw one come inside with her.

"Yeah, I thought about it, and the Sea Cows may be able to get on base. They did before."

"Oh. Smart thinking. Guess I should do the same," Robby said.

"Anything new from Vickers?" Alex asked.

Robby ignored her. "How's Jack?"

"How's the sex with your massage therapist?" Alex went for the shock factor. She said it loud enough for the others in the office to hear her.

Kimberly A. Biggerstaff © 2024

"All right, not so loud. He said he'd call me with anything new. Are you keeping on our kid Collins?"

"Yeah. I think I'm going to talk to his coworkers and supervisor. But I think he was just . . . unlucky," Alex said, looking at her computer. She felt really bad that this kid might have been killed just to send a message to her. "If they took those photos of me on set, why didn't they just kill me then?"

"Good question," Robby said. "What if they're using you as a distraction?"

Alex looked at him. She picked up her phone and called Jack. "Dammit, voice mail. Jack, listen to me. I want you to get security. Hurting you might be how they hurt me." She hung up and looked at her guy. "Call whoever and get protection on Jack Hailey. He's the guy that hired you for us."

"Yes, ma'am. Is there a threat we need to know about?"

"No, but he's . . . close to me. You understand?"

"Yes, ma'am." The man was older than Alex but was respectful. And knowing she was a federal agent, he took her at her word. She didn't know it, but he had been US Army

Special Forces. When he got out of the service he went to the ISA Academy, an executive security school, where he learned to be a bodyguard. "Do you know where he is right now, ma'am?"

"No. Check the studio," Alex said. "They may be filming on another set and can't have phones. I'll keep calling him."

"Yes, ma'am."

It was nearly noon when Alex's phone rang.

"Where the hell are you? Are you okay?" she yelled at Jack.

"Hey, I'm fine. What's the matter?" he asked.

Alex took a deep breath when another agent looked at her from across the room. "I've been worried about you. Robby had an idea that maybe they'd try to go after someone close to me to hurt me. I want you to have protection too. Just in case. Where are you, Jack?"

"I'm in Des Moines," he told her.

"What are you . . . oh. His family is there." Alex realized he had flown to Des Moines, Iowa, to see the family of Airman Collins.

"Yeah. I need to pay my respects. He was working on my lot, my picture. I should have told you, I'm sorry. It was a last-minute thing."

"I understand. I would have gone with you if you had told me," Alex said.

"I'm still at the airport. I'll be careful, Alex. It's nice to know you're worried about me"

"No, stay there. Let me make a few calls. I might be able to get someone to go with you."

"Alex, I can—"

Alex interrupted him. "Jack, no. We're not taking any chances. Stay there. I'll call you back."

"Yes, ma'am," Jack said, hanging up.

"We have anyone near Des Moines?" Alex asked Robby.

"Just call the local PD. Have them send an officer."

Alex did just that. She was passed around on the phone and finally reached someone who would help. "Look, I just need one officer to watch his back. Probably less than twenty-four hours."

"Who are you again?"

Alex sighed. "I'm Agent Alex Yates with the Air Force Office of Special Investigations out of MacDill Air Force Base, Tampa, Florida. I'm a federal agent." She was getting frustrated.

"Yeah, I know what OSI is. I was Security Forces for four years."

"One officer just until I can get someone else there."

"Sure, I'll send someone. Give me his information."

"Thank you." Alex sighed in relief and provided him with the details. She phoned Jack back.

"Hello."

"Local PD is sending an officer to go with you. Be careful, Jack, and call me when they get to you. In fact I want you to call me or text every hour."

"Alex isn't that—"

"Just do it!" she yelled and hung up.

Robby looked at her from his desk. She was getting stressed, and he needed to calm her down. He glanced over at the lieutenant colonel's office. The door was open, and he knew she was in there. He was surprised she didn't make an appearance. She had to have heard Alex yell.

"Hey, take a break, Alex. Come on, let's go to lunch," Robby suggested. "I'll buy."

She looked at him. "Yeah, I guess I could use a break. And if you're buying I have to go."

"Don't get used to it," he told her.

Robby told their CO they were going to lunch. "Robby, close the door," she said.

"Yes, ma'am."

"How is she doing?" his boss asked.

"Putting on a good front. She doesn't like being sidelined. But none of us would."

"What about Hailey?"

Kimberly A. Biggerstaff © 2024

"Uh, what do you mean, ma'am?" Robby said but knowing what she was asking.

"It was my understanding they haven't been involved for a while." She paused and added, "I just need to know where her head is at. I don't care who she dates."

"Um, yes, ma'am. They broke up while she was still filming. But I believe things have changed recently. He went to Iowa to pay his respects to Collins's family. I was going to brief you that we think the Sea Cows could target him to get to her."

"The photo. They know they're involved."

"Well, they broke up soon after that, but this case has thrown them together again."

"I see. Well, keep an eye on her, and keep me informed," Lieutenant Colonel Barrett said.

"Yes, ma'am." Robby gave her the status of the case from what Vickers had told him about an hour ago. "Uh, ma'am. How long are you going to be with us?"

"Tired of me already, Robertson?" she asked, smiling.

Kimberly A. Biggerstaff © 2024

"No, ma'am. I think we can learn a lot from you."

"This is a temporary duty for me. I need some command experience before moving to my next assignment."

"How do you like Tampa?"

"It's fine. The weather is similar to San Antonio. But there's a lot more water, and I'm not fond of boats."

"Is there a story there, ma'am?" Robby asked.

"Maybe."

"What's your next assignment, do you know?" he asked.

"Aviano."

"Nice. I loved Europe. I was at Ramstein for a tour."

"My first base was in Germany," she told him. "Anything else, Robertson?"

"Any words of advice on how to handle a female rookie?"

"A female rookie?" She was almost offended.

"I didn't mean it like that. She's like a little sister to me. We've been together for a couple of years now. That first case was . . . well, she got thrown in the deep end." He looked at his boss and added, "I read about your first case. The one with the Russian. You got thrown in the deep end first time out as well."

"First OSI case, yes. Maybe tomorrow we'll talk. Go to lunch," she said, and he turned to leave. Then the CO called to him, "Don't let her shoot you, Robertson."

"There's only two people I would trust to shoot me: Yates and you, Colonel Barrett." He smiled and opened the office door and went to Alex.

Alex was waiting by the main door and asked him, "Is she worried about me?"

"Yes. But I reassured her you're okay. She asked about you and Jack. I had to tell her."

"It's okay. She probably saw the photo, right?"

"It's evidence. But it's a copy, and it seems someone sanitized it," he said coyly. Vickers had sent them copies of everything, including the photos. But when the photo of Alex and him arrived there was black tape over her chest and their middle area. It was obvious what they were doing, but Robby appreciated the fact that Vickers had taken the time to do that.

"You're such a good partner."

"I'd like the credit, but it wasn't me. Thank Vickers. Jack's a lucky guy; you have a nice set of—"

"Robby!" she said, getting in the car. "Thank you." She smiled at the compliment. She was used to his sense of humor. He made her laugh and was a really good partner. "I feel like a Cuban sandwich."

"Sounds good. Tampa Sandwich Shop?"

She smiled as she drove. "You know it."

"Colonel Barrett is interesting, isn't she?" Alex said. "She just put the silver oak leaf on, right?"

"Yeah. So what? She's just getting her command experience and then she'll move on," Robby said.

"Oh. What's up? You want to date her?" Alex asked him. She was just messing with him, but if he said yes, she could have fun with that.

Kimberly A. Biggerstaff © 2024

"What? No. She's . . . you know." He looked over at her as she drove. "You really don't know anything about her?"

Alex was quiet.

"First of all, she's married . . . to a woman. Although I think she was once married to a man. He was killed by an IED so she's a Gold Star Wife. Second of all, that's Samantha Barrett. They use some of her cases at FLETC. She earned the Silver Star in Afghanistan. You can learn a lot from her. Rumor has it she sometimes does work for the CIA."

Alex was again quiet. She knew perfectly well who Samantha Barrett was. She just wanted to hear what Robby had to say about her.

*****

After a long day of searching for a connection between Collins and the Sea Cows, Alex was exhausted. Jack checked in as she requested.

"You sound tired," Jack said. "Why don't you go to my place and relax? Swim or sit in the hot tub. There's a sauna just off the gym. I'll be back in a few hours. In fact, pack a bag and stay with me."

"That sounds nice. How do I get in?"

Alex told Robby her plans. Jack had given her his new alarm code and that he had a spare key hidden. Being a former cop, the key would not be easy to find. He reminded her to set the alarm once inside. She told Robby she'd see him later and went to her apartment to pack a suitcase and get Brutto. After they arrived at Jack's house, one security guy went inside with her and the other stayed outside.

Alex looked at Brutto and said, "I'm going for a swim, boy." She changed into her suit and jumped in the pool. Brutto ran around the edge, and then he finally jumped in and swam to her. "Brutto, I didn't know you liked to swim," she laughed. He went to the steps and got out and shook the water off. "One lap and you're done?" He barked and she laughed again. He rolled over on the warm concrete and lay there. Alex swam a few laps and got out. There was an outdoor kitchen and bar.

She went to the fridge and, looking at the beer, she hesitated and went with a glass of wine instead. She lay down on one of the lounge chairs. It was eight o'clock and getting dark.

Suddenly Brutto got up and growled, looking out into the yard. "What is it, boy? A squirrel? Rabbit?" Alex didn't see anything but wasn't comfortable, so she got up and went inside and locked the door. She went back and checked the alarm.

"Hey, Fred?" she said to the security guy.

"Yes, ma'am?"

"Would you mind having your partner check the backyard? Brutto heard something. It might have been an animal, but . . . it would make me feel better."

"No problem." He called his partner and told him to check the backyard. A few minutes later Fred's phone rang. "Yeah, okay."

"What's wrong?" Alex asked.

"He found some footprints but that was all. He's doing another check. I'll call and get another guy so we'll have one for the back and front."

Kimberly A. Biggerstaff © 2024

"Did you learn that from your training? What's your background?" Alex asked.

"Special Forces, ma'am, and I attended a protection school. Most of us are former military or cops," Fred said.

"Okay. I feel a little better. Thank you, Fred. I'm going to bed."

"Yes, ma'am. Let me sweep the top floor. Then I'll stay down here."

"Sounds good."

Fred did an extensive and thorough search of the second level and then came back downstairs. "All clear, Ms. Yates. I'll sweep this floor again too. Good night."

"Mr. Hailey is out of town but should be coming home tonight. It'll be late," Alex told him.

"Yes, ma'am. I'll let our relief know," Fred told her.

She smiled and went upstairs to Jack's bedroom. Brutto followed close behind. Having the dog made her feel a little safer too. She placed her handgun in the nightstand drawer next to the bed. Then she changed her mind and placed it under her pillow.

*****

Brutto lifted his head and began to growl softly. Alex suddenly yelled, "Brutto, sic balls." And Brutto leaped at the figure.

"No, Alex, it's me. Brutto, out!" Jack yelled as he covered his balls and turned from the dog's teeth. "Ow. Alex!"

"Brutto, alto," Alex said, sitting up and pointing her weapon at Jack. Brutto went back to Alex and jumped on the bed next to her.

"I was hoping to make a more discreet entrance," Jack said, looking at his hands.

"I'm sorry. I'm just a little on edge."

"I guess that's better than the alternative," he said. "They said they found footprints out back."

"Yeah. Brutto is great. I wasn't sure if it was an animal or not. But when they found footprints, I went on alert. I'm sorry. He didn't hurt you, did he?"

"You taught him to bite ankles and balls?"
Kimberly A. Biggerstaff © 2024

"I'm a single woman in a city," Alex said. "Come here. Maybe I should check you out." She smiled at him.

"He might have drawn blood," Jack said.

"Let me examine you, Mr. Hailey."

Jack began to undress while keeping an eye on Brutto. He left his briefs on and carefully crawled into bed.

"Brutto, down. Go to your bed," Alex said, and the dog jumped off the bed and went to a doggy bed on her side next to the wall. He grabbed a toy in his mouth and squeaked it. "Good boy."

Alex put her arms around Jack and they kissed. "I'm glad he's alert and makes you feel safe," Jack told her.

"You make me feel safe too," Alex said as she snuggled close in his arms.

CHAPTER 8

Alex woke early and wanted to go for a run. She changed and went downstairs.

"Morning, Fred. Is it possible for me to go for a run?"

"Let me change and I'll go with you, ma'am," he told her. He went to their SUV and retrieved his bag.

"Morning," Jack said, coming into the kitchen. "Going for a run?"

"Yes. I'm waiting on Fred. He's going with me."

"Good." He gave her a kiss. "Have a good run." He placed his hands on her waist and felt her weapon. "Do you always run with that?"

"Not always, but I am now. What are you going to do?" Alex asked.

"Work out in the gym. Lift day. I've been slacking a little."

"You look fine to me," she said, admiring his chest before he threw on a tank top.

Fred appeared in his running gear. "Ready, ma'am." His weapon was in a belly band under his shirt. He had his radio, phone, and a small medical kit in a backpack slung over his shoulder. He clicked the mic on one of the backpack straps and said, "Rabbit One, radio check."

"Read you loud and clear, Rabbit," a voice said.

"Wow, all these hot men around. What will I do?" Alex said, glancing at Fred.

"Take care of her, Fred," Jack said. "I mean keep her safe."

Alex smiled as she got the reaction she wanted from Jack.

"Yes, sir," Fred said as he clicked the mic again. "Rabbit and Tigger on the run," he said as they left. Jack watched as Brutto sat by the door.

Kimberly A. Biggerstaff © 2024

"Did she feed you?" Jack asked the dog, who came back and looked at him. He walked to the kitchen where Brutto's bowl was and saw it was empty. Brutto practically flipped it over. He texted Alex. Feed Ugly?

No. Go ahead.

"Here you go, boy." Jack put some dog food in his bowl and gave him fresh water. Then he went to get his mail. One envelope caught his attention. He dropped it on the counter and picked up his phone. "Robby. I got an interesting piece of mail. You need to get over here." Jack didn't want to open it or touch it any more until Robby arrived. Vickers arrived first.

"Agent Robertson said you had some mail?" the detective asked.

"Over here on the counter. I set it down and haven't touched it," Jack told him.

Vickers looked at it. It was a letter-size envelope with a few manatee stickers on it. The ones the Sea Cows used but smaller. Robby arrived and joined them.

"Manatees," Robby said, sighing.

"Well, let's see what's inside." Vickers said, putting on latex gloves and picking up the envelope.

"Wait, what if there's . . . anthrax or something in there?" Jack said.

"Anthrax?" Vickers looked at him. "Okay, we'll take it back to the station and open it under safe conditions."

"Where's Alex?" Robby asked Jack.

"She went for a run. With protection," Jack said. "Want me to get her back?"

"Yes," Vickers said.

Jack called her, and it didn't take long for her to come running inside. "What's happened? Jack, are you all right?" She ran to him and hugged him.

"Yeah, I'm fine. I was going through my mail, and this was with it." He pointed at the envelope Vickers had.

Kimberly A. Biggerstaff © 2024

"The Sea Cows. Open it," Alex said.

"No, not here. We don't know what's in it," Jack told her.

"Give it to me," Alex said, holding her hand out.

"No. It's addressed to me," Jack said. "You might be right and they might want to—"

"That's not their style. They would shoot us out on the street. Poisoning is not what they would do," she said.

Jack started to speak but then looked at Vickers when he heard the envelope opening.

"Dammit, Vickers!" Jack yelled.

"She's right. Gangs don't poison." He pulled out a piece of paper and a photo.

The paper had letters glued to it. They were cut out from magazines and such. They formed one word: "CHEATER."

The photo was of Jack and another woman in bed, and it had a date on it. Yesterday's date.

Kimberly A. Biggerstaff © 2024

Alex looked at Jack. She slapped him and went upstairs to pack her things. The men looked at Jack, who didn't say anything. Alex came back down with her suitcase. "Brutto."

Jack covered his balls.

"Brutto, ankles." And the dog began to bite Jack's ankles. As soon as he moved his hands, Alex said, "Sic balls." And Brutto snapped at him.

"Brutto, alto!" Jack said. "Dammit, ow. Alex, let me . . . ow." But Brutto kept snapping at him. He got his thighs a few times. "Shit. Alex, please."

The men were watching and cringing. One of the police officers instinctively covered his balls.

"Brutto, alto. Come, boy." Alex opened the door and left with Fred trying to stay ahead and keep watch.

Jack had scratches and bites on his ankles and groin area. He was wearing shorts, so it made it easier for Brutto.

"I knew you were an ass," Robby said, leaving. Vickers put the letter and photo back in the envelope and left with his

Kimberly A. Biggerstaff © 2024

men. Jack was left standing there with blood running down one leg into his sneaker.

When he finally snapped out of the daze he was in, he went to one of the hall bathrooms and changed into his swim trunks. He jumped in the pool and started doing laps. Lap after lap after lap until his arms were so sore he could barely move them.

*****

Alex drove to her apartment and ran upstairs, slamming the door behind her almost forgetting Brutto was there. He yelped when his tail almost caught in the door. Alex looked back at him. She sat on the floor, grabbing him and hugging him as the tears began flowing.

There was a knock at the door. But Alex didn't move.

"Alex, it's me," Robby said. "Let me in." He waited. "Please, sis."

Alex got up and wiped her eyes. She opened the door for Robby and let him in. As soon as he came inside, Alex hugged him and cried again.

Kimberly A. Biggerstaff © 2024

"I'm here, sweetie. I'm here," Robby said, holding her.

CHAPTER 9

It was near the end of the week when Alex was called into her CO's office.

"Have a seat, Yates. How are you doing?" Sam asked as she took her seat behind her desk.

"Fine, ma'am. How are you?"

Sam smiled and replied, "Fine. How's the case?"

"I'm not on the case, ma'am, other than running background on Collins and talking to his coworkers. I didn't find any connection to the Sea Cows."

"Yes, I saw your report. You know I had a case once I called Operation Nine Iron."

"Yes, ma'am. The staff sergeant killed on the golf course." Alex smiled while leaning forward, ready to listen to her.

"Yes. You're familiar with it?"

"I may have read a few of your cases," Alex said.

Sam turned away and rolled her eyes. *Why do they read my cases?* she thought. She turned back to face her. "Then you know we initially thought it might be a subordinate or someone she gave a hard time to."

"Yes, ma'am. But then—"

"Yates," Sam interrupted her. "Let me tell it."

"Sorry, ma'am." She sat back in the chair.

"You kind of ruined it. Did you read all my cases?"

"Sorry, ma'am. I think so. The OSI ones."

Sam sighed. "Tell me how it ended. The Nine Iron case."

"You realized that men could be abused too, and when you reinterviewed that senior airman, he admitted it was his boyfriend who took revenge for what the female staff sergeant did to him."

"Yes. We were looking at things from the wrong point of view."

"I don't understand what you're trying to tell me, ma'am," Alex said.

"Just think about it. I saw the photo of Mr. Hailey and sent it to a contact of mine. Well, actually it was my wife's contact. I thought you'd want to know that the photo was manipulated and the time stamp was faked."

"The photo was faked?"

"Yes. Never jump to conclusions, Yates. Understood?"

Alex looked down. "Yes, ma'am." She was disappointed in herself. "How could I think . . . I let my emotions cloud my judgment."

"And try to think of other perspectives." Sam could tell Alex felt bad, and she looked defeated. "You're a good agent, Yates. You just need experience. That's why I wanted you to take lead on this case."

Kimberly A. Biggerstaff © 2024

"Yes, ma'am," Alex said.

"Come back after you have something," Sam said, closing the folder. "Dismissed."

"Ma'am, am I back on as lead agent?" Alex asked.

"Not until you come back with something," Sam said.

Alex stood up and went to her desk.

"Why the glum look?" Robby asked.

"I jumped the gun. The photo was a fake," Alex told him.

"What? How do you know that? Did Vickers call you?" Robby felt like he was suddenly out of the loop.

"The boss used a contact," Alex said. "Why did she tell me about that case? The staff sergeant, the senior airman, the boyfriend." Alex started talking it through. "It doesn't make sense. Men can be abused too."

Robby sat and looked at her while she mumbled to herself. "What are you talking about? Alex?"

"Shhh. Don't distract me. I'm trying . . ." She sat taller in her chair. "Hot damn! A distraction. That's it, Robby. I was a distraction. This isn't about me or the Sea Cows."

"What?" Robby was confused as ever. He didn't have a clue what she was talking about. "What do you mean it's not about you or the Cows?"

Alex smiled and stood up. "Wow, she is unbelievable. So smart." Alex went to Sam's office and knocked on the doorframe.

"It's not about me. I was a distraction. It's been about Jack this whole time," Alex said.

"I suggest you contact Detective Vickers. He'll want this report on the photo from the lead agent on the case." Sam wasn't looking at her. She was looking at her computer as she pushed the folder forward on her desk.

Alex smiled. "Thank you, ma'am." Alex took the folder and went back to her desk.

"Mind filling me in?" Robby said, getting frustrated.

"Yeah, we need to see Vickers. I'll tell you on the way."

*****

Jack went back to work. He kept the security because Vickers told him that he might have been the target all along. He also told him that the OSI gave him evidence that the photo was fake. Jack had mixed feelings about that. He knew the photo was fake, but Alex didn't even give him a chance to explain. He was glad they learned the truth, but he was also still mad that he wasn't even given a chance to deny it.

"Mr. Hailey, here's your coffee," Addy said.

"Thank you, Addy. Where do you get this? It's really good."

"It's just something a friend sends me from up north," she said, smiling at him.

"Well, thank you," Jack said.

"Mr. Hailey, if you need any help with anything, just let me know."

Kimberly A. Biggerstaff © 2024

He smiled and she left. Jack went over to one of the soundstages to see how the movie was progressing. "Ron, how's it going?"

"Everything's fine. We're catching up, and we should finish on time. Maybe even under budget."

"Good. Very good."

"Are you okay? You look a little tired," Ron said.

"I'm fine," he said. But he had been feeling a little off lately. He went back to his office and sat down. He checked his calendar to see what he had coming up. In a few weeks he had a red-carpet event for one of the movies they were releasing. His plan was to ask Alex to go with him, but now he thought about going alone.

*****

The next morning Jack came in and Addy was waiting for him. "Here's your coffee, sir."

"Thank you, Addy." She started to leave, but he stopped her. "Addy, would you like to be my PA?"

Addy jumped at the chance. "Yes, sir."
Kimberly A. Biggerstaff © 2024

"Good. I'll give you my schedule," he said.

*****

One Saturday, Addy knocked on his door.

"What are you doing here?" Jack was more than surprised to see his personal assistant at his home. The security guard had called and asked if she was okay to come up to the house.

"I brought some paperwork for you."

"Oh, well, you didn't have to bring it to my house."

"Is Jackson Jr. your name?"

"What?" he took the folder but didn't respond.

She repeated her question. "Is Jackson Jr. your name?"

He looked up at her with a blank face.

"Jackson Jr.," she said.

"Yes, Addy," Jack said.

"You asked me to bring the paperwork and said you'd show me your home. I also brought some coffee for you."

He was confused. "I . . . uh . . . must have forgotten."

"Yes."

Kimberly A. Biggerstaff © 2024

"Come in," he said. He showed her around the house and asked if she wanted a drink.

"Yes, thank you. I brought this wine."

"Okay." They went to the kitchen and Jack retrieved two glasses.

"Please, let me," she said, pouring the wine. "May I call you Jack?"

"Yes," he said quietly. He felt a little different. His head was swimming.

Addy brought the glass to him. "To friends," she toasted.

"Friends," he said. He sipped the wine. "Mmm. Very good. Has a familiar taste."

"I'm glad you like it," she said. "I'm enjoying being your assistant, Jack."

"You're doing a fine job," he said. They sat and talked for a while.

"Have some more wine, Jackson Jr."

"Why . . . do you . . ." He wanted to ask a question but he couldn't.

"Have some more wine, Jackson Jr."

"Yes. I'd like some more wine," Jack said.

They finished the bottle and Jack was falling asleep.

"Are you tired, Jack?"

"Mmm, yes. Tired. Don't feel . . . I should go . . . lie down." He went to stand but was very unsteady.

"Let me help you, Jack," Addy said. She helped him stand, and they walked upstairs.

"I don't know why . . . I'm so . . . tired," Jack said.

"It's probably stress, Jackson Jr."

"Stress. I must be tired due to stress," he said. "My room."

Addy helped him to his room, and he collapsed on the bed. "How do you feel, Jack?"

"I feel . . . good. Relaxed but tired," he said.

"Let's get you into bed." Addy sat him up and took his shirt off. Then she removed his shoes and socks and pants. "Get into bed, baby."

"Into bed."

Addy looked at him lying there in bed. "I can come over tomorrow, if you like?"

"Hmm? No . . . that's—"

"Jackson Jr., you'd like me to come over, wouldn't you?"

"Yes. Come over tomorrow," he said.

"Good night, Jack." She gave him a kiss on the cheek and left.

*****

"Have you seen Jack?" Ron Ford asked Jack's secretary.

"No, sir," she said.

Jack had been going to the office less often. Or he'd go and leave early. Ron called him, but Addy always answered. *He's working from home. He's at an appointment.* That's what Addy would tell them.

Kimberly A. Biggerstaff © 2024

"Addy, more coffee?" Jack asked.

"Of course. Here you go," she said, pouring him a cup. "Jack, the red-carpet event is in a few days. I'd like to go."

"Will you go with me to the opening of the movie?" Jack asked.

"Yes, honey, I'd love to. Thank you. You have some paperwork to sign."

"Okay." He smiled at her. They worked for a while and then went for a swim. That evening they were drinking wine, and Addy leaned over and kissed him.

"I . . ." Jack started to talk but didn't know what he wanted to say.

"Shh, it's okay, Jackson Jr. You love me."

"I love you, Addy."

She stood up and took his hand. He stood and looked at her, waiting for her to tell him what to do. She stepped close and looked into eyes. "You love me, Jack. I love you."

"I . . . love you."

Addy grabbed the wine and his glass, "Take me to your bedroom, Jack."

He took her hand and led her upstairs to his room. They stood near the bed. "Kiss me, Jack," she said.

He kissed her, and then he asked her, "More wine, please?"

"A little, honey," Addy told him. "Try this chocolate first." She opened a box of chocolates she had brought up earlier and placed a piece in his mouth.

"Hmm. Good."

"Yes, Jackson Jr., the chocolate is good." She kissed him again and took his shirt off. "You are a very handsome man," she said as she ran her hands over his smooth, muscular chest. "Jackson Jr., make love to me."

Jack kissed her and slowly undressed her. He moved her bra strap and kissed her on the shoulder. Then he reached around and removed her bra, kissing her on the other shoulder. He took her panties off and picked her up and laid her on the bed. Then he removed his pants, but he stood there.

"Jackson Jr., come here, honey." Addy held out her hand, but he didn't move. She gave him another piece of chocolate. "It's okay, baby. I love you and you love me." She took his hand and placed it on her hip. "You want to make love to me, Jackson Jr. You love me."

"I love you," he said. "Thirsty," he said. "May I have some wine and more chocolate?" he asked.

"Yes. But I wouldn't want you getting dehydrated." She went to her bag and gave him a bottle of water. He took a few sips.

"Tastes . . . funny."

"It's fine. Have some wine and a piece of chocolate," she said, giving them to him. "Now that I gave you what you wanted, you want to make love to me, right, Jackson Jr.?"

"Yes." He took his briefs off, took her hand, and they lay on the bed.

"I love you, Jack. How do you feel?"

"Relaxed."

"Good, relaxed is good." Addy smiled and kissed him. "Make love to me, Jackson Jr."

He moved his hand to her neck and gently leaned in for a kiss. He was gentle and took his time, exploring her body. But then Addy took control.

*****

Addy held him tight. "Jackson Jr., that was wonderful. You're a wonderful lover."

"I'm a wonderful lover," Jack said.

Addy pushed him over. "Here. Since you were so good, you earned a piece of chocolate." She fed him a piece.

"Mmm. I'm tired."

"Okay, Jackson Jr., let's go to sleep." Addy covered them and snuggled in his arms, and they fell asleep.

*****

The next morning Ron drove over to Jack's. He told security who he was, and he was cleared to proceed. He knocked and rang the bell. Finally, after ten minutes Addy answered the door.

Kimberly A. Biggerstaff © 2024

"Where's Jack? And what the hell are you doing here?" Ron asked.

"I'm his personal assistant and his girlfriend," she said, cinching her robe.

"Girlfriend? Where is he?"

"Ford, I'm here," Jack said, walking to the door in a robe.

Ron looked into his eyes. They looked glassy, and he seemed different. "Are you drunk? Or high?"

"No, I'm fine. Relaxed," Jack said. "What do you want?"

"I want you to come to work," Ron told him.

"The studio is fine. Addy is a great assistant. Everything is under control." He placed his arm around her waist and kissed her.

Ron narrowed his eyes and said, "Can I talk to you alone?"

"No. I'm fine. You can go."

"She's a little young for you, don't you think?" Ron asked.

"You can go," Jack said. "We'll see you at the premiere."

"So you are going?"

"Yes, we'll be there," Jack said. He looked at Addy and kissed her again.

Ron didn't know what to think. Something was wrong, but he couldn't do anything right then, so he left.

CHAPTER 10

The case was going nowhere. Vickers and his partner were frustrated, and so were Alex and Robby. "Let's go over it again," Vickers said to his partner, John Rich. They were interrupted by a call from Alex.

"Any luck finding the shooter?" she asked.

"No. They were careful. No prints or anything to identify them. What about you?"

"Nothing. Maybe Robby and I should reinterview everyone that was on set again. Either this person works there or got through security somehow."

"Be my guest. I'm out of ideas," Vickers said.

"Come on, Robby. Let's go to the studio."

"Okay," Robby said, following her.

They drove to the studio and went to Jack's office first.

"Hi, Mrs. Troy. We need to see Mr. Hailey," Alex said.

"Uh, he's not here," she said.

Ron came in. "Alex. Robby. I'm so glad to see you. The gate called and said you were coming."

"Is something wrong? We'd like to reinterview everyone," Alex said. She could tell something was bothering him.

"Sure, talk to anyone you need. Come into Jack's office." They went inside and Ron closed the door. "Something is wrong with Jack."

"What do you mean?" Robby asked.

"First of all, I heard about the photo and you guys. I'm sorry. But you need to talk to him."

"The photo is a fake. Our boss had it analyzed, and it was manipulated," Alex told him. "I . . . should have given him the benefit of the doubt. My mistake."

"You need to talk to him," Ron repeated. "At least go see him. He's acting strange."

Kimberly A. Biggerstaff © 2024

"He's an ass," Robby said. He had no problems saying how he felt. Anyone who hurt Alex physically or emotionally was an ass. If Robby could have gotten away with it, he would have punched him.

"Robby, the photo was a fake." Alex looked at Ron. "What do you mean 'strange'?"

"If I didn't know better I'd think he was high or something. But he'd never take drugs. He's not like that. And he has a zero-tolerance policy on set or anywhere on the grounds."

"Well, Alex, maybe you messed with his head," Robby suggested.

"There's something else. He made Addy his PA and is . . ."

"Is what?" Robby asked.

"Dating her."

"Addy? My PA?" Alex laughed. "She's not his type, and what is she? Twenty?"

Ron was serious as he said, "She's practically living with him. He rarely comes into the office anymore. She's got some kind of hold on him."

"I don't care who he dates," Alex said nonchalantly. But the truth was that she was worried about him.

"Alex, please. At least go have a look for yourself. Please. I'm worried about him." Ron grabbed her hand. "Please."

Alex saw the pain and fear for his friend in his eyes. "Okay, we'll go see him," she said. "After we interview everyone here."

*****

"Jackson Jr., look at the dress I bought for the premiere," Addy said, twirling around. "What do you think?"

"It's . . . beautiful."

"Like me?"

"Like you. Beautiful," Jack said, smiling. "Can I have some chocolate or wine, baby?"

Kimberly A. Biggerstaff © 2024

"Yes. Let me change," she said. "Unzip me." She turned so he could unzip her. "Kiss my neck, Jackson Jr."

He did what she said, and she pulled her arms through the dress. She walked over to the closet and hung the evening gown up. She turned and looked at him. "You look like you're losing weight, getting a little soft. When was the last time you worked out?"

"I . . . don't . . . know," he said. "Tired."

"I need to take better care of you. I'm sorry, honey." She walked over to him. Jack was sitting on the bed in his briefs. "Do you still love me?"

"I love you, Addy," he said. "Thirsty. May I have a drink?"

"Yes, baby. Stay here." She smiled at him, touching his face and giving him a kiss. She went to the bathroom and got him some water. "Have some water," she said when she came back.

"No, wine, please."

"Drink some water first, Jackson Jr. Then you can earn the wine."

"Water first." He smiled and drank it all.

"Better?"

"Better."

"Good boy. Tomorrow we'll work out in the gym."

"Tomorrow we'll work out," he said.

Addy ran her hand through his hair. "You need a haircut and a shave too, baby."

"Haircut and a shave." He smiled.

"I'll get someone to come out." She pulled his head to her stomach as she stood there in her underwear.

"Wine?" he asked.

"You have to earn it. How do you earn it, Jackson Jr.?"

"I have to earn it." He pulled her panties down and kissed her stomach. He stood and walked around so he was behind her. He kissed her neck, shoulders, and back. Then he turned her around and gently pushed her down on the bed. He knelt and spread her legs as he kissed her thighs. He lightly bit her and continued kissing her. He teased her and then he made her climax. She gripped the sheets and relaxed when it was over.

"Oh, Jackson Jr., you are wonderful."

"I'm wonderful," he said.

Addy sat up and ran her hands through his hair. "I love you."

"Did I earn . . . my wine?"

"I love you, Jackson Jr.," she said. "I wish I didn't have to . . ." She stopped talking.

He smiled. "I love you, Addy."

"Now you earned it," she said. She put her panties on and stood up. "Shall we go downstairs?"

"Downstairs for wine."

"Yes, baby." She kissed him, then handed him his robe and put hers on. "Come on, lover." She took his hand and they went downstairs. Addy fixed the wine and handed him his glass. He drank it quickly. "Jackson Jr., I told you not to do that. Now you have to wait." She took him to another room, and they lay on the couch. Addy lay down first and pulled Jack down to her, holding him. "How do you feel, honey?"

"Fine. Never better."

"Good boy." Addy smiled, running her hands through his hair. "Jack, tomorrow we'll go out and buy an engagement ring. You want to marry me, Jackson Jr."

"I . . . want to marry you," he said, closing his eyes.

Addy smiled and closed her eyes. They lay there for a while, and then Jack got up.

"Where are you going, Jackson Jr.?"

"I have to pee," he said.

"Hurry back," she said.

Jack did his business and came back. "I want more . . . need to earn it. I'll make love to you," he said.

"Not yet, honey, it's too soon. You need some water, sweetheart." Addy got up and took his hand to get some water. "Drink some water. I think we'll go work out now. I need to give you something to do."

*****

Kimberly A. Biggerstaff © 2024

The interviews yielded nothing new. They'd have to hunt down some people who weren't there. After the last interview Robby asked Alex, "So do we go to Jack's?"

"I said we would check on him, so we will."

They parked on a side street and walked to the front door, where they were stopped by security. "This is an official welfare check. We're federal agents," Alex said as they showed their badges. She didn't recognize the man. Probably a new shift was on or different personnel.

"Sorry, ma'am. No visitors today."

"I don't think you heard me. We're federal agents doing a welfare check. You can't stop us," Alex said, pushing her way past him. She rang the doorbell, but no one answered. Alex banged on the door. She looked at the security guy. "Call him."

"Her."

"What?" Alex asked.

"Ms. Parker said to call her with any questions or problems."

Kimberly A. Biggerstaff © 2024

"Fine, call her."

He phoned Addy. "She said no visitors, not even you."

"Get the fuck out of the way or I'll arrest you," Robby yelled. "Try the door."

"Wait. Call her back and tell her Agent Robertson wants to see Jack and talk to him. Otherwise we'll come in one way or another," Alex said.

The guy called Addy back. "She said give them ten minutes or so. Agent Robertson can go in."

"Fine." Alex looked at her watch.

Eleven minutes later she was about to say something when the guy's phone rang.

"She said to escort you in, sir."

"Whatever. Go." Robby was pissed. They went inside. Jack was sitting with Addy next to him. They were holding hands. He was wearing a polo shirt and pants. She had jeans and what looked like one of his dress shirts on.

"Jack, you need a haircut," Robby said.

"Yes, we've been busy. He'll get one tomorrow and a trim for his beard. Right, honey?" Addy said.

"Yes, haircut and trim the beard," Jack said.

"How are you doing?" Robby asked him.

"I feel fine. Never better." He looked at Addy and kissed her.

"Why haven't you been at work, Jack?"

"Addy's my PA. She brings me any paperwork. The studio is fine. She's doing a fine job."

"May I speak to you alone?" Robby asked him.

"No, you can say anything in front of Addy."

"Fine. Stand up and walk over here."

"No. I'm fine. Never better," Jack said.

Robby walked over to him and looked into his eyes. "What are you taking?"

"Nothing," he said. "You need to go. I need to earn my wine." Jack ran his hand up Addy's leg.

"Jack, you need to come with me," Robby said.

"You need to go. I need to make love to Addy." He took his shirt off and pulled his oversize shirt over her head.

"Unless you want to watch I suggest you leave," Addy said as he kissed her neck.

Robby stood there to see if he'd really go through with it. When Jack took his pants off, Robby turned away. "There's something wrong, Jack. You need help."

Addy whispered in Jack's ear. Jack turned and repeated what she said. "You need to leave or I'll fuck you too."

He touched Robby on the ass. "Goddamn it," Robby said and left.

"Come here, baby," Addy said, and Jack undressed her.

Robby came out and looked at Alex. "He's on something. Narcotics probably. But there's something else. The way he was talking was strange. He looked a little thin. Needs a haircut and shave."

"Let's arrest him on suspicion of—" Alex said, moving toward the door.

Robby grabbed her arm. "No. I don't want you going in there. Let's just leave for now," he said.

"No, we can—"

"Alex, he's in there screwing her. Undressed right in front of me."

Alex turned and started toward the car. Suddenly she went to a planter and kicked it over. Then she went back to the car and got in.

"Feel better?" Robby asked.

"No."

*****

"You did great, baby," Addy told him.

"I want to make you happy so you'll give me my reward," Jack said, kissing her breast. They made love, and Addy brought him some water and wine.

"Sip it, honey. Make it last, Jackson Jr."

"Make it last," he said, taking the glass.

*****

Kimberly A. Biggerstaff © 2024

Alex had multiple emotions running through her. She was angry, jealous, and sad. She still cared about Jack and didn't like what Robby said. She mumbled to herself the entire way back to base. She slammed her desk drawer and threw a stress ball across the room. It almost hit Sam, who was coming down the hall from the break room. She cleared her throat and looked at Alex.

"Yates, with me," she said, turning around.

"Shit," Alex said quietly. She stood up and followed her CO down the hall. They went outside, and Sam set her coffee down. She went over to the wall of the building and picked up a bat. She handed it to Alex and pointed to a clearing barrel. The red barrel was elevated at an angle and secured to the cement floor of the patio. It was filled with sand but had a hole in the middle to point a weapon muzzle into. This is where military members would clear their weapons. It was a safety measure to ensure any accidental discharges (when loading and unloading weapons) went into the barrel and not somewhere else.

Alex approached the barrel with the bat. "Ma'am, I apologize."

"Hit it," Sam said.

"I'm okay. I just—"

"Hit it now. That's an order."

Alex held the bat and looked at the barrel and swung. It was a weak swing.

"Again," Sam said.

Alex swung again a little harder. Sam looked at her, and Alex swung again and again, each time harder, until she put her full weight into it. She finally stopped and dropped the bat.

Sam picked the bat up and put it back against the wall. Then she went back inside. Robby came out a minute later.

"Wow. Did you do that?" he asked.

"Yeah."

"She told me to tell you to get your shit together and trust your gut," Robby said. "That was a direct quote."

Alex took a deep breath. "You were right, Robby. I can learn a lot from her." She cracked a slight smile, and they went inside. Alex sat down at her desk.

"Addy is behind this, Robby. I know it."

"Well, let's see if we can find something. We don't have anything else and neither does Vickers," Robby said.

"I'll run background," Alex said.

"I'll let Vickers know."

"Would you call Ford first and let him know you saw Jack," Alex asked.

"Sure."

CHAPTER 11

Alex let out a growl of frustration. "Need some swings?" Robby asked.

"No. Just a break." She stood up and walked to the break room. She had run background on Addy but couldn't find anything or any connection to anyone on set. She had an alibi, so she couldn't have pulled the trigger herself. "What is your endgame? To get Jack for yourself? Take his company? Marry him? Go back to the beginning. I was dating Jack. We kept it quiet, but she knew and took photos. Someone took a photo of us in the trailer. Jack was on the floor, and she came to the door. Did she know he was there? Did she take the photos?" Alex walked back to her desk. She opened the folder and looked at the photo of her and Jack. She looked at the angle it was taken from. "Robby, did Vickers find out how this photo was taken?"

"You mean was there a peephole or something?"

"Yeah," Alex confirmed.

"No. No peephole."

"And they didn't find a camera?"

"No," Robby said.

"Spy cameras. Spy camera detectors." Alex smiled and stood up and went to Sam's office and knocked.

"Come in."

"Ma'am, do you have access to a hidden camera detector?"

Sam smiled and retrieved something from her go bag. She walked over to Alex and handed it to her. "This will locate cameras and bugs. I want that back."

"Yes, ma'am. Thank you."

"Robby, let's go," Alex said to him. She didn't expect her boss to have one with her, but it sped up the process.

"What is that?"

Kimberly A. Biggerstaff © 2024

"A hidden camera and bug detector."

"Cool. Let me see it. Wait. The boss had that with her?"

"Yeah."

"Well, that's kind of scary. I knew she worked for that other agency," Robby said, happy he was right.

"I'll buy you an ice cream," Alex said. They drove back to the studio and found Ron. He gave them permission to do what they needed. Alex turned on the device and walked around. It went off immediately in Jack's office.

"Shit," Ron said.

"Shh." Alex walked over to the small refrigerator and looked behind it. She found a bug. She pointed to it and put a finger to her lips, telling them not to say anything. It was the only one in the room, so they left. The outer office was clean. They went to the trailer that was Alex's during filming. The detector lit up when she opened the door. Alex walked over to a table and looked at the object.

"It's a pen," Robby said.

"Not just any pen." Alex put her gloves on and picked it up carefully. She put it in an evidence bag.

"Don't you need a search warrant?" Ron asked. "It's been months."

Robby held up a piece of paper.

"Oh, okay," Ron said.

They found one more pen in the trailer and bagged it, as well. They went to the soundstage and walked around but didn't find anything.

"Well, we'll take what we have and see if we can get anything from it."

"How was Jack?" Ron asked.

"I thought Robby called you," Alex said.

"He did. I want to hear it again."

"I think he's on drugs. He didn't look good. Lost a little weight. Needs a haircut and shave. She's doing something to him," Robby told him again.

Ron shook his head. "We need to do something. If she marries him or gets him to sign something turning over his control of the studio . . . I have a twenty-five percent stake in the studio. Jack has the other seventy-five percent."

"We're working as fast as we can within the law," Abby said.

"They're going to the premiere of a movie we have coming out."

"When?"

"A week from Saturday. At the CMX Hyde Park. Would you two like to go?"

"Oh, I don't know," Alex said.

Robby jumped at the chance. "Yes."

"It'll be good practice for when your movie comes out," Ron told her.

Alex smiled. "Oh . . . okay. I guess I'll have to get a dress. Come on, Robby. Let's figure out who these belong to," she said holding the evidence bags. Trying to give Ron some hope she looked at him and winked. "Hang in there, Ron,"

CHAPTER 12

They were leaving the property when they stopped at the gate.

"Got what you need, Agents?" the guard asked.

"Alex," Robby quietly said and looked down at the detector going off. He had forgotten to turn it off. Alex looked at it and then at the guard.

"Hey, that's a nice pen," she said, noticing the pen in his pocket. "My little brother is graduating high school, and maybe a pen set would be good. Along with other stuff. Where did you get it?"

"Oh, uh, I can't remember. I've had it awhile."

Robby opened his door and got out while Alex put the car into park.

"What's going on?" the guard asked.

"We need you to come with us," Robby said, walking around the front of the car.

He stepped back. "Why?"

"We just have some questions."

"Look, I didn't do anything."

"Then come with us and just answer some questions. We're talking to everyone."

The guard was starting to panic. Sweat began to form under his cap and roll down his cheek. He looked around and then ran toward some buildings.

"Shit." Robby ran after him.

Alex turned the car off and ran after them. The guard ran down an alley, opened a door on the side of a building, and went inside. Robby followed, drawing his weapon and carefully opening the door. Alex caught up and backed him up. Jack was going to renovate the building, so it was dark and under construction. Alex had drawn her weapon as well, and they carefully began clearing rooms. "This will take us forever," Alex whispered. "Call Vickers."

Robby reached for his phone and placed it on silent. Alex did too. "Dead spot," he whispered, seeing no bars on the phone. They heard footsteps and pointed their weapons in that direction. Alex went first down the hall. They were halfway down the hall when they heard a shot and the door they had come through opened and closed. Robby ran to it and followed the guard outside. The guard turned his weapon toward Robby as he ran and fired. Robby returned fire, hitting him in the back. He fell and Robby caught up to him.

"You better say your peace," Robby said as he tried to stop the bleeding.

"It was for fun." He coughed and gagged. "We . . . played . . . spy . . . when . . . kids. Didn't . . . know . . ." He let out a breath. His last breath. Robby checked him, but there was no pulse. He took an evidence bag from inside his jacket pocket, and with a handkerchief he placed the weapon in the bag.

"Alex!" he called. No answer. No sign of her. "Shit!" He ran back to the building and saw Alex lying on the floor.

Kimberly A. Biggerstaff © 2024

"Alex. Oh my God." He saw the blood coming from her side. "Come on, sis." He picked her up and carried her outside to a place where he hoped his phone would work. He set her down, taking his handkerchief out and pressing it to her wound. She yelled.

"Hang in there, Alex. Dammit! Still no signal. We have to get farther away from this building. Come on." He helped her up.

"Robby, stop. I'm okay."

"No, come on, you can make it." He had his arm around her.

"Get off! I'm fine." She pushed him away. "See, it's a scratch." She lifted her shirt. "A ceiling tile hit me on the head and knocked me out."

He stared at her. Then his face went hard and he turned and walked away.

"Robby." Alex chased him. "Hey. Talk to me. Stop." Robby kept walking, so Alex grabbed his arm to face her. "Thank you. I'm okay."

"Whatever," he said. "That's not a scratch, but it's not bad. You need to clean it." They walked up to the body.

"Dammit. What happened?" Alex asked.

"He shot at me. He also said some things." Robby told her what he said.

"Where's the weapon?"

"Right here. I bagged it." He patted his jacket pocket. "What's next . . . boss?"

"You call Vickers and an ambulance. I'll call our boss," Alex said.

They waited for Vickers and the locals to arrive. Vickers had his officers secure the scene and let Alex and Robby give their statements.

"Uh-oh," Robby said.

"What?" Alex asked.

"The boss is here." He nodded at the car approaching.

"So. Our last boss came in the field."

Kimberly A. Biggerstaff © 2024

"I know, but I have a feeling it's different with her," Robby said. "So what do you think? Is she going to yell at us or walk silently up and then walk away?"

"She'll do that walk tall silent thing. I wish I was tall like her," Alex said.

"You're fine. And you carry yourself like you're six feet tall."

"Aww, thanks, partner."

Sam showed her credentials and spoke to Vickers for a while.

"What did she say on the phone?" Robby asked.

"Not much. Just asked if we were hurt."

"She's kind of a hands-off commander. It's nice not having someone looking over our shoulders all the time. But she still has a way of teaching you," Robby said.

"Shut up. Here she comes," Alex said, elbowing him in the gut.

Sam walked over to the body and looked at it. The guard was face down. She knelt down, scanning him. She saw something on his arm.

"What's she doing?" Alex asked.

They watched as Sam put gloves on and carefully lifted the guard's short sleeve so she could get a better look at the tattoo. She sighed and then looked at Robby and Alex. Reaching into her suit jacket pocket, she took out her phone and snapped a few photos of the tattoo. Sam stood up and whispered something to Vickers before walking over to Alex and Robby.

"Good work. But you aren't finished," she said, and then she looked at Yates. "Get your head checked." Then she saw the small patch of blood on her shirt. "Get that taken care of too."

"I'm fine ma'am. It's just a bump." But Sam gave her a look that scared the crap out of her. "Yes, ma'am." Alex walked over to the ambulance and had a paramedic check her out.

"Turn the suspect's weapon over to Vickers," Sam said to Robby. "Give me your weapon. You're on desk duty pending an investigation."

"It was a good shoot, ma'am," he said, checking his weapon and placing it in the bag she held.

"I know. Get back to base. Take your car. Run the guard," she told him. She showed him the photo. "Know what that is?"

"A military tattoo. Army? Not sure, ma'am."

"British SAS. Check his records," Sam told him. "Call this number if you have any problems with his military records." She handed him a card.

Robby walked past Sam and looked at Alex and mouthed the word "scary." Then he walked back to the gate and got in the car and drove it back to base.

Sam walked over to the paramedic. "I'm her boss. What's her status?"

"She's fine. Just a bad bump. No signs of a concussion. But if she has headaches or any vomiting, get to a doctor," the paramedic said.

"I'm very familiar with the protocols," Sam said. Alex stood up from where she was sitting on the back of the ambulance. "With me," Sam said. They walked over to the body. "What got this started?"

"We found a bug in Mr. Hailey's office. And this camera pen was in the trailer that I used when I was working. We were leaving, but Robby didn't turn the detector off. It went off at the gate while talking to the guard. I saw a similar pen in his shirt pocket."

The medical examiner arrived, and Sam asked if she could look at the front of his shirt. He nodded and Sam looked and sighed again. "No pen," she said.

"Shit. He dumped it. Probably in there." Alex nodded at the building they'd chased him through. "I swear he had a pen like this one, ma'am."

Sam walked to her car and went in the trunk. She came back with another detector.

"You have two, ma'am?" Alex asked, surprised.

"You're wearing an ankle holster as a backup, aren't you?" Sam said.

"Yes, ma'am."

"Always be ready Yates." They went into the building and started searching. Eventually there was a weak signal on the detector. They found a room and began to look. The signal was intermittent. "He may have tried to destroy it."

"Found it." Alex smiled, picking it up with gloves on. She placed it in an evidence bag and they left. They briefed Vickers, who said they could run with the pen. They'd take it back and have forensics go over it. When they got to Sam's car, Alex automatically went to the driver's door.

Sam tossed her the keys and got into the passenger side. Alex was surprised she didn't say anything about driving.

CHAPTER 13

After riding along for a few minutes Sam asked, "So what happened?"

"Ma'am?"

"What traumatic experience happened that makes it necessary for you to drive all the time?"

"It was long ago. I'd rather not talk about it."

"Take a left at the light."

"But base is . . . yes, ma'am," Yates said.

After another minute Sam spoke again. "You know when I came back from my deployment to Afghanistan I had a hard time. There was a lot that I couldn't remember due to the blast. I've had a few concussions. The scars are hard enough to deal with. But not being able to remember was ruining my marriage. I had done something I wasn't proud of but couldn't remember what it was. I finally went to therapy and remembered what I did that was affecting my . . . personal relationship with my wife. I told her right away, but she didn't forgive me right away. We went to counseling, and eventually she forgave me and we worked through it. There's nothing wrong with getting help. I've finally realized that. If something affects your life negatively, you should try and fix it."

Yates was quiet. She listened. She was surprised that Lieutenant Colonel Barrett would share something so personal with her.

"Mr. Hailey is a good-looking guy. Reminds me a little of my husband without the beard," Sam said.

"Husband?"

"I was married to a man. He was killed by an IED."

"I'm sorry, ma'am."

She followed the directions Sam gave her and was surprised when they pulled into a parking lot for Chuck E. Cheese's. "Hope you like pizza," Sam said, getting out.

Kimberly A. Biggerstaff © 2024

They went inside and Sam looked around. She smiled and went toward a booth. A little boy with dark hair ran up to her and hugged her.

"Hi, Commander."

"Hi, Caleb. Did you guys order already?" She picked the boy up and smiled at him.

"Yes, ma'am. Is this one of your troops?" he asked.

"Yes, this is Agent Yates. This is my son, Caleb," Sam said, putting him down.

"Hi," Caleb said, looking at her.

"Hello," Alex said.

Sam walked to the booth and slid in. "Have a seat, Alex." Sam leaned over and kissed the blonde-haired woman smiling at her. "Agent Alex Yates, this is my wife, Katrina Davis, and our daughter, Quinn. Agent Alex Yates."

"Uh, hello," Alex said. "Nice to meet you, ma'am."

"Hi, please sit down," Katrina said. She looked at Sam and said, "You didn't tell her you were coming here."

"No."

"Do you have any stories?" Quinn asked Alex.

"Stories?"

"Yes. I'm going to be a writer and write a book about mommy and the commander's stories."

"Oh. Well, one of my stories is being made into a movie," Alex said.

"No way!" Caleb said.

"Cool! Can you tell me?" Quinn asked.

"Maybe later, Quinn," Sam told her. "Where's Lex?"

"Becoming King of the Games," Caleb said. Their pizza arrived, and Sam sent Caleb to get his brother.

"Commander, I got . . . oh, hello." Lex switched to speaking Russian. "You're a very beautiful lady. What's your name?" he asked, smiling at her.

"Excuse me?" Alex didn't understand what he said in Russian. All of this was a bit overwhelming.

"Lex, stop flirting. You're ten years old," Katrina said.

Sam laughed. "This is our other son, Alexi. Or Lex. He said you're a very beautiful lady and asked your name."

Kimberly A. Biggerstaff © 2024

"Alex Yates and thank you," she said. "Was that Russian?"

"Yes, ma'am. My father is Russian."

"The commander can speak any language. Ask her," Quinn said proudly.

"Yeah, try and stump her," Caleb said.

"Hungarian," Alex said.

"Yes, I can speak Hungarian and many others," Sam said in Hungarian.

"Another one," Caleb said. It was a game for the kids. No one could stump Sam. It was a gift. Alex tried a few more, but Sam said something in each language. Then she looked at the kids.

"How do we know she's really speaking those languages and not tricking us?"

"Because the commander has integ . . . integrity," Lex said proudly, remembering the word.

"Thank you, Lex. Is that your word of the day?" Sam said, rubbing the top of his head.

Lex laughed. They ate their pizza and the kids asked Alex questions. Then they ran off to play more games.

"You eat too much pizza. I'll bet that's all you eat when we're not here," Katrina told Sam.

"Well, you're here now for the week, so you get to keep me in check." Sam smiled. "Did her partner call you yet?"

"No. Should he?" Katrina asked.

"Maybe. Well, I guess I should go teach Lex a thing or two. I was telling Alex about the time I cheated on you in the sandbox. Discuss." Sam left to find Lex.

"Um, she never told me she cheated," Alex said, a little embarrassed.

"She didn't go all the way. But still. You don't have to be embarrassed. I'm glad she's more comfortable talking about. So how many stories has she told you?"

"I guess that was the second. She doesn't say much to us. I mean she does when she needs to."

"Taking a laissez-faire approach. Interesting. So what was the first story she told?"

Kimberly A. Biggerstaff © 2024

"Operation Nine Iron. But I read all her cases so I knew about it. She used it as a distraction to make me think outside the box."

"And this one?" Katrina asked.

"She told me a personal story."

"Why do you think she would share that?"

Alex sighed. "Because I have a personal issue I don't like to talk about. And it sometimes affects my relationships with others."

"Hmm. She sometimes does that with the kids. I wondered how she'd be as a commanding officer. She would fill in for her CO back in San Antonio, but this is her first on her own. Is she doing okay otherwise?"

"Yes, ma'am. She's great."

"Would you tell me if she wasn't?" Katrina gave her a slight smile.

"Probably not. But we really do like having her as our CO. It's an honor to be working for someone like her." Alex hesitated and then said, "She's different away from the job. I mean just coming here, she's like a different person."

"Yes. It's why I've been coming to see her once a month. Long weekends I bring the kids."

Katrina's phone rang. "Excuse me. Hello? Yes, Agent Robertson, my wife said you might call. Yes. Colonel Barrett is my wife. How can I help? British SAS and the name. No, that's all I need. I'll get back to you."

"You work for the agency, don't you," Alex said quietly.

"Yes. And I consult for a few other three-lettered ones. That way I can be home for the kids. I don't go in the field anymore if I can help it."

Sam appeared. "Well, if you're finished we should get back."

"What's wrong, Lex?" Katrina asked the boy, who had a sour look on his face.

"The commander beat me every time," he said sadly.

"You won't get better if I let you win," Sam told him. "Someday you'll be King of the Games. But for now I am." She rubbed his head. "Besides, you beat Caleb all the time. Ready, Yates?"

"Yes, ma'am," Yates said, standing. "Nice meeting you."

"Hey, are you leaving?" Caleb asked, running over. Quinn walked over too.

Alex smiled at the kids. "Yes, we have to get back to work. Or I do. I have a case to solve."

"Okay. Don't let the commander shoot you," Lex said.

"Hey, I did that to save his life. And he's fine. Hit him in the love handle. His wife thanked me," she teased.

"She did not. Don't tell them that, Sam," Katrina said.

"Never shoot anyone unless it's self-defense or in the defense of others," Lex told Alex.

"Hey, she didn't show us her badge. You have to show us your badge," Caleb said standing in front of her.

"I do? Why is that?" Alex asked.

"Because there's spies that lie about what they do," Caleb whispered.

"Oh. Here you go." She showed it to him.

"Okay. Thank you, Agent Yates." He saluted her.

"You don't need to salute me."

"Are you enlisted?"

"I'm not supposed to say, but yes. Just an enlisted grunt," Alex said quietly.

"Don't say that," Lex told her. "All troops are important. You probably work harder than most of the officers. Except for the commander."

Alex smiled. "Thank you, Lex."

"Okay, let's go," Katrina said. Sam kissed her and they left.

Alex paused when they approached the car. Sam had gone straight to the passenger side. Alex stared at the seat. Sam gave her a minute and then started to say something but kept quiet.

Alex wanted to explain to Sam. "You know on the set one day he told the director to put me in the passenger seat. I did try but . . ."

"Jack?"

"Yes. I couldn't do it. Called him a bastard and punched him."

"I won't force you. I know what that's like, and I wouldn't do that. You'll know when the time is right. Although therapy helps. Up to you."

Alex went to the driver's side and slid into the seat. "Back to base?"

"No, take me to Jack's."

"Oh, yes, ma'am." Alex didn't know what her game plan was.

"So, tell me about this girl."

"Addy? She's about twenty. She was my PA, but I didn't really give her anything to do until Jack and I broke up and he told me to get a dog. I had her find me a dog trainer, and she helped take Brutto there."

Kimberly A. Biggerstaff © 2024

"Brutto."

"It means Ugly in Italian. An inside joke with Jack." Alex smiled sightly thinking about it.

"Uh-huh. And she didn't seem to have any interest in Jack?"

"Not that I noticed. Jack and I were discreet the first time. I didn't think anyone knew."

"Jack paid for the security?"

"Yes. Until recently. But now that we know it's not the Sea Cows I guess that's okay."

"Still, don't get too relaxed," Sam told her.

Alex pointed. "That's the house. Access to the driveway is in the back on a side street."

"Okay, drive around so I can get a look."

Alex turned left from Bayshore Boulevard down a side street, then she took another left. "That's his driveway and garage." She slowed but kept going. And took another left. She stopped at the corner. "Ma'am?"

"Ugh. Go around and park on that first side street. I don't want to stop on Bayshore. Park where we can watch the front," she told Alex.

When they got close Alex parked where they had a view of the house. It wasn't ideal, but it would do. "Nice house. Nice view of the bay," Sam commented.

"It's a nice house. It was his father's, and when he passed Jack bought his sister's half. May I ask why your kids call you 'commander'?"

"Two moms gets confusing. When Lex was little we played a game. I was his commanding officer and he was my executive officer. My lieutenant. Commanding officer to CO to commander, and that stuck."

"That's sweet," Alex said. "Ma'am," she added. Alex felt that might have been inappropriate. "I'm sorry."

"Why? It's fine. They're great kids. Katrina had Lex when she was married. They came to live with me when he was eight months old. We used a donor for the twins, and Katrina carried them."

"Is it difficult being . . . I mean in the service . . . never mind. It's none of my business."

"What, being gay or bisexual or whatever? I was never attracted to a woman until I met Katrina. It was strange at first. I mean I just never made a point of being . . . you know. I'm a little more comfortable about it." Sam stretched and looked at the limo that had stopped out front on Bayshore. "Oh, I guess they went out."

Alex was agitated. "A limo? Spending all his money. Of course she's probably got him too doped up to drive." She sighed. "Ma'am, I don't understand why we're here."

Sam texted someone. Twenty-five minutes later a car pulled up behind them. Katrina walked to them. "I'm here. What's going on?"

"A little undercover work," Sam said.

Katrina smiled. "I thought we did that at home."

"Alex, would you watch the kids for a few minutes?"

"Sam, you're the CO. She has a partner," Katrina reminded her.

"He's on desk duty. Shot a guy and killed him. It was a good shoot."

"So you're taking over?"

"No. I just want some more information, and they know her."

Katrina sighed. "Fine, what's the plan?"

"You think Addy would be interested in women?" Sam asked Alex.

"No. I never saw anything that would lead me to believe that," Alex said. "The goons won't let you in."

"Men? Where?" Katrina asked.

Alex pointed. "Over there."

"We can get by them. Then what?" Katrina asked.

"We need to talk to this guy and the girl," Sam said. "I want your opinion."

"Okay. Watch the kids, Alex. We'll be back," Katrina said.

Sam took off her jacket and unbuttoned her shirt so her cleavage was showing. "Let me see the new earrings."

"What new earrings?"

"You didn't go shopping?" Sam said sarcastically.

Katrina smiled and walked back to the SUV. "Lex, hand me that bag." She took the earrings out and went back to Sam. "You know me so well."

Sam looked at the earrings and put them on. "Pretty. Probably cost more than a month's salary," she teased.

Alex smiled at their interaction. Sam gave her holstered weapon to Alex. "Are you carrying?" she asked Katrina.

Katrina gave her a look.

"That's my girl. You're so hot." Sam unbuttoned Katrina's shirt and messed her hair. "Maybe when—"

"Let's go, Samantha. I have laundry to do." Katrina began walking.

Alex walked over to Katrina's SUV, and Lex put the window down halfway. "Are we on a stakeout? Are Mom and the commander going undercover?" Lex asked quietly.

"Ask them when they get back."

"That means yes!" Caleb yelled.

Kimberly A. Biggerstaff © 2024

"Shh, quiet, you dingbat. You have to be quiet on a stakeout," Lex told him.

"Be nice, guys," Alex said as she watched Katrina and Sam go up to the house. She glanced at Quinn, who was writing in a notebook. The men stopped Katrina and Sam.

"I'm telling you this is it. Addy said the party was here. We're early," Sam told her.

"Ma'am, you can't go in."

"What? Addy invited us. And don't call me ma'am," Sam said, smiling at him.

"What's your name?" Katrina asked the other man. They flirted and started touching the men. Before long they opened the door for them and let them in.

"Who the fuck are you and how did you get in?" Addy said.

"It's me, Sam. Jack invited us over to party."

"No he didn't. I've been with him for weeks."

"Well, it was a while ago at that premiere or after-party. I can't remember," Katrina said.

"Jack! Jack sweetie, where are you?" Sam called out.

"I'm here," Jack said, appearing. He was in nothing but his briefs.

"Jack. We came to party," Katrina said, going to him.

"Party?"

"You invited us. You said whenever we were back in town to look you up."

"I want you to leave," Addy said.

"Jack honey, all of us can party." Katrina started putting her hands on him. Jack just stood there and let her.

"I have wine. We have to earn it," he said, beginning to unbutton Katrina's shirt.

"Don't forget me, Jacky." Sam went to him and began kissing him. "How do we earn the wine, baby?" she asked, running her hands over his bare chest between kisses.

"Make love," Jack said, kissing her neck.

"Jackson Jr., you need to stop and they need to leave," Addy told him angrily.

"We need to stop and you need to leave." He stopped and stood still.

"Jack. Come with us. I have wine," Katrina said.

"No, Jackson, they need to go or you'll call the police."

"You need to go or I'll call the police."

"I'd love some wine, Jackson Jr.," Sam said, kissing him.

"In the kitchen."

"No! Get out!" Addy yelled.

"Let's make love and drink wine," Jack said, grabbing Katrina and kissing her.

"Jack, what happened at the studio? We went there and cops were all over the place. Some guard got killed, I think," Sam said.

Addy's face went blank. "What? What guard?"

"I don't know. We left and came here," Sam answered.

"Who did it?" Addy asked.

"Some female cop."

"Alex," Addy said quietly.

Kimberly A. Biggerstaff © 2024

"No, it was . . . Barrett, I think, Agent Barrett I heard someone say," Sam said.

"No. No, it can't be true," Addy said. She needed to get rid of them. "Jackson Jr., go upstairs and wait for me, baby. I love you."

"I love you, Addy," he said and he let Katrina go and went upstairs.

"Fine, this blows. We'll go to a club," Sam said. "Come here, sweetie." She grabbed Katrina and kissed her a long time while sticking her hand in her shirt and feeling her breast. "You are so hot. Let's do it in the car."

"Let's ask George to join us." Katrina winked at her.

"Get the fuck out!" Addy yelled.

"George, want to join us?" Katrina asked the guard at the door.

George smiled. "I get off at ten."

"I'm getting off in five minutes," Sam told him with a wink and a smile. They walked out the door, and Sam pulled Katrina around the corner.

"Sam?"

"Just a quickie. I'm all wound up now."

*****

"So what happened?" Alex asked when they returned.

"He's definitely on something. She's using some sort of conditioned response. 'Jackson Jr.' is his key word," Katrina told them.

"Do I get like that when I flip out?" Sam asked.

"No. Not quite."

"Why did you tell her you shot the guard?" Katrina asked.

"To see what she'll do, and I didn't want to put Robby or Alex at risk."

"Mommy, I'm tired of staking out," Caleb said.

"Stop whining," Lex told him.

"Are we done?" Katrina asked.

Sam kissed her. "Yes, you are finished. Thank you for your help."

"Mommy and the commander sitting in a tree . . ." Caleb starting singing the song.

"Caleb. Stop," Quinn said. "It's romance," she said dreamily.

"Wow," Alex said to herself and got out of the SUV and let Katrina get in.

"See you later," Katrina said. "Thank you, Alex."

"No problem," she said, and Katrina drove off.

Alex and Sam went to their car and got in. "I hope the kids were okay," Sam said.

"Yeah, they were fine. You and your wife are something else, ma'am."

"Is that good or bad?"

"Where did you go after you came out of the house?" Alex asked.

Sam smiled. "I got a little worked up and had to release some . . . energy."

"Oh." Then Alex realized what she meant. "Ohhh. Right there? Really?"

Sam laughed. "If you only knew. Back to base."

CHAPTER 14

Sam walked in and went to Robby. "What did you learn?"

"The guard, James Patrick Thomas, was born in Tampa. Parents were killed in a home break-in. He was sent to a relative in England. Still waiting on stuff from England. He moved back here five years ago and began working as a guard at the studio."

"Officer Davis will get back to you. She was with us," Sam said. "Keep me informed."

"What have you been doing?" Robby asked Alex after Sam went back to her office.

"We went to lunch. I met her wife and kids and then we went to Jack's. She and her wife went in to see Jack."

"Any change?"

"No. Officer Davis said he's on drugs and Addy's using some kind of controlled response on him."

"What, like hypnosis or something?"

"I guess, I don't know. I learned a lot about the colonel. She's very interesting," Alex said.

"What's her wife like?"

"You'd like her. She's a very pretty blonde-haired, blue-eyed woman," Alex told him. "They make a nice couple. They both were married to men."

"Yeah, I told you I thought she was a Gold Star Wife."

"I can confirm she is," Alex said.

"So what are you, best buds now that I'm sidelined?" Robby asked.

"You'll always be my partner, Robby. Don't be jealous," Alex said. "We have to find a way to get Addy away from Jack."

*****

The next day Sam walked in and handed Robby a folder.

"From Officer Davis," she said.

Kimberly A. Biggerstaff © 2024

"Thank you, ma'am," he said, taking it and opening the folder. "When he was seventeen he joined the British Army and eventually the SAS. Medical discharge."

"But what brought him back?" Alex asked.

"You know when I get stuck I lay everything out so I can see it," Sam said from her office door. She took a sip of coffee and then went back to her desk.

Alex closed the folder she had and took it to an interview room. She brought in a whiteboard and began attaching the papers on it with magnets. "Robby!"

"Here you go," he said, bringing more magnets and dry-erase markers.

"There has to be a connection. The colonel told me Addy got upset when she mentioned the guard being killed. We need to find the connection. Why would she kill Collins? Jack and I were broken up. She could have made her move then."

The board was against the far wall with an interview table between it and two chairs. After staring at the board Alex sat down in a chair. Robby sat next to her. They didn't speak for half an hour. They just sat staring at the board, pictures, and notes they made.

"I need a break. Come on, I'll buy you a coffee and candy," Alex told Robby.

While they were in the break room, Sam went to the interview room and looked at the board.

After Robby and Alex took their break they went back to the interview room and stared at the board again. Behind them Sam stood in the doorway drinking a coffee. After a few minutes she said, "You know when I was a kid we lived in a villa in Italy. A lot of land and woods. Neighbors weren't very close. Had to play with my brother a lot."

Alex and Robby jumped when she started speaking. They were concentrating so hard they didn't know she was there. Sam went back to her office.

"What the hell does that mean?" Robby said.

"She saw something. She's helping us."

"Lived in a villa? Is her family rich?"

Alex talked it through. "No neighbors. Played with her brother."

"No. Could Addy and James be related?" Robby asked. They looked through the papers. "No."

"Wait. Neighbors! Where did they live? Tell me Addy's addresses."

Robby read off her addresses up until eighteen years of age. Then he read where James lived.

"That's it. They were neighbors! For three years." Alex gave Robby a kiss and a hug.

"Hey, I can report you for sexual harassment," he said. "James said they played spies as kids. Of course we didn't know who he was talking about. That's probably why he had the pen. It's thin but a little closer. Good work, Yates."

"Let's see if Vickers has searched his place yet." Alex called Vickers and told him that the guard and Addy lived next door to each other when they were kids.

"I was just going over there. Care to meet us?" Vickers asked.

"Yes. See you soon," Alex said, hanging up. She went to Sam's office. "Ma'am, we're going to the guard's home. Vickers is on his way over there too."

"Okay."

Alex began to walk away and hesitated. She looked back at Sam. "Would you like to come, ma'am?"

"Yes." Sam stood and caught up with them.

"You can ride shotgun, ma'am," Robby told her.

"Have you been cleared of the shooting?" Sam asked.

"Oh man," Robby said, going back inside.

Sam smiled. "Been there. It sucks."

They drove to James's address. "Are you fricking kidding me?" Sam said as they approached the marina.

"Ma'am?"

Sam sighed. "I'm not fond of boats."

Alex didn't say anything as she parked the car. They walked out on the slip to the large boat. "I think this is technically a yacht," Alex told her.

"I don't care what it's called. It's on the water."
Kimberly A. Biggerstaff © 2024

"So, I'm not the only one with an issue."

"I have a lot of issues, Agent Yates. Don't be insubordinate," Sam told her.

"Sorry, ma'am." Obviously this bothered Sam a lot. Alex couldn't blame her. After all, she punched Jack for trying to mess with her issue.

"Agents. Welcome aboard," Vickers greeted them as they approached. He held out a hand to assist Alex onto the yacht.

"Find anything?" Alex asked.

"Not yet," he said and then he waited for Sam, holding his hand out. "Agent Barrett?"

"What?" Sam stood there with her arms crossed.

"Coming aboard?"

"Just go ahead," Sam said as she let out a breath and wiped her brow.

Vickers shrugged and took Alex below to check out the living and sleeping quarters. "She get seasick or something?" he asked.

"I don't know." Alex shrugged and put on some latex gloves. Vickers's partner was already looking through the guard's things.

"Hey, Vickers," Detective Rich said. "Take a look at this." He held up a photo book and gave it to Vickers. He flipped through it as Alex looked over his shoulder. There were photos of James and Addy as kids. They were the usual birthday and playing around type of photos. But as Vickers flipped through the photos, more recent ones were just of Addy. A few were taken on his yacht, but more at the studio.

"Find something?" Sam said, appearing and not looking well.

"Yeah, this photo book. Are you okay?" Vickers asked.

Sam had one gloved hand on the nearby table. "And?"

"Looks like he might have been wanting to be more than friends now that she was older."

Sam suddenly bolted for the door and got off the boat.

Kimberly A. Biggerstaff © 2024

"Give me a minute," Alex said. She went to check on Sam, who was breathing hard and kicking a pylon on the dock. "Are you okay, ma'am?"

"I'm . . . fine," she said, looking at her dress boot, which now had a few nice scuffs in the leather. "Dammit. Get back down there."

"Yes, ma'am." Alex understood. She didn't have to know the details to understand the fear or pain or whatever it was with Sam.

A few minutes later Sam yelled, "Vickers!"

"Does she yell a lot?" he asked Alex.

"Not really," Alex said. "She mostly left us alone to do our job until Robby shot James."

Vickers went back up onto the dock. "Agent?"

"Did you run financials yet? How can he afford this boat?" Sam asked, trying to take deep breaths and calm herself.

"Life insurance from his parents. He couldn't access it until he was eighteen. He's been very frugal. He also gets military medical disability from the Brits."

Kimberly A. Biggerstaff © 2024

Sam nodded and Vickers went back below. Sam mumbled to herself, thinking about the case while cursing herself about the boat. She kicked the pylon again and walked closer to the yacht and grabbed the handrail. Taking a deep breath, she started to come aboard but Alex stopped her.

"That's not necessary, ma'am. We're finished for now," Alex told her. Vickers and his partner followed Alex off the yacht.

"Finished?" Sam asked.

"He didn't have a lot. But we found these keys to a storage unit," Vickers said.

"Are they labeled?"

"Found a business card. I'll get a warrant and call you," Vickers told them.

Sam began walking to the car. She got in and slammed the door. Alex gave her a second and then slid into the driver's seat. "Back to base?"

"Yes."

It was a quiet ride until Alex finally said, "I'll tell you mine if you tell me yours."

"What?"

"I'll tell you about why I have to drive if you tell me about the boat."

Sam huffed. "No. Just drive."

"Yes, ma'am." Alex didn't say anything else. When they arrived back at the office, Sam went to her office and slammed the door closed.

"What happened?" Robby asked.

"She has an issue with boats."

"Yeah, she mentioned it briefly when I asked how she liked it here. So?"

"James Thomas lived on a boat. Actually it's a yacht. Big and nice. He probably used the life insurance from his parents' deaths to buy it."

"Did she—"

"Robertson!" Sam yelled.

He jumped up and went to her office. His weapon was on her desk. "Take that and get back to work. You're cleared," Sam said gruffly.

"Thank you, ma'am," Robby said, taking the holstered weapon. He left her office and closed the door behind him.

"That was kind of quick," Alex said.

"Yeah. But I'm not complaining. Wow, I'd hate to be her wife when she gets mad," he whispered.

CHAPTER 15

Alex briefed Robby on what they found on the yacht. They were catching up on some paperwork when a young boy burst into the room. He ran over to Alex and standing at attention said, "Ma'am, Alexi Rogov reporting as ordered."

"Hello, Lex. At ease."

"Alexi Rogov!" The rest of what Katrina said was in Russian, and Alex smiled.

"Sorry for running in," Lex told Alex.

"Well, it's nice to see you again."

"Hi, Agent," Caleb said, running up to her. "Is this your desk?"

"Hi, Alex," Quinn said.

"Stay away from her desk. She might have important things on it," Katrina told them.

"Nothing top secret. Still working a case or two," Alex said.

Caleb went over to Robby and said, "Hi. I'm Agent Barrett."

"No, Agent Barrett is in her office," he said, pointing to the door. Caleb laughed at him.

"Agent Robertson, this is Officer Katrina Davis and Lex, Caleb, and Quinn. My partner, Agent Robertson."

"Nice to meet you, ma'am," Robby said, standing and going to shake her hand. "Thank you for the information you sent."

"Good to meet you too. Glad I could help. Is she busy?"

"Uh, I don't know," Robby said.

Katrina saw his face change and asked, "Did something happen?"

"We went to search a suspect's . . . yacht," Alex explained.

"Oh. Did she go on it?"

"For about five minutes," Alex said.

"Oh man. Wish I could have seen that. I've never been able to get her on the water. I don't know why she hates boats."

"Do you have games on your computer?" Caleb asked Robby as he spun in his chair.

"Caleb, stop spinning," Katrina said.

"Sorry, Mommy," Caleb said as he stopped spinning. He looked at the things on the desk. "Do you have any toys?" He started to open a drawer, but Robby stopped him.

"That's my top-secret drawer. All my cool toys are in there. But don't tell Alex," Robby whispered.

"Would you guys like a tour?" Alex offered.

"Yeah!" they all said.

"Best behavior, troops, or it's the brig," Katrina told them. "Thank you."

"The brig is Navy, Mom," Lex said.

Alex smiled and took Caleb and Quinn's hands. Lex followed with Robby.

Katrina knocked on Sam's door. "Not now!" Sam yelled. Katrina sighed and texted her. Sam opened the door.

"What are you doing here?"

"The kids wanted to see your office. Alex is giving them a tour."

"Hmm."

"Nice office."

"It's okay." Sam was disappointed in herself.

"Maybe you should call your psychiatrist or your CO back in San Antonio. Get some insight or help." Katrina suggested.

Sam got angry. "Why? Did she tell you there was a boat?"

"Why are you getting upset, Sam?"

"I'm supposed to be a leader. This is a steppingstone to Aviano. To my first command of a detachment."

"You're not perfect. You've been through a lot," Katrina said.

"I never said I was perfect. I know I have flaws and that I'll make mistakes. But I—" Katrina walked over and kissed her.

"What was that for?" Sam asked.

"For admitting you have flaws."

"Very funny." Sam wrapped her arms around her waist. "How can I tell her to confront her issue when I can't do the same?" she said softly.

"I don't know," Katrina said. "Seems a bit hypocritical. I still don't know what your problem is with boats."

"Let's forget about the boat."

"I want to take the kids out to see the dolphins."

"Good, do that while I'm working." Sam kissed her and began moving a hand under her shirt.

"Sam, we're in your office."

She smiled. "Yeah. I'll lock the door."

*****

"You don't want to appear weak in front of your troops, right?" Katrina asked, straightening her blouse.

Kimberly A. Biggerstaff © 2024

"Maybe."

"Well, maybe that will let them see you are human."

Sam sighed as she fixed her belt. "I guess."

"She admires and looks up to you. Maybe showing her you're human will be good for her. You won't lose her respect as long as you talk to her. Don't make her do anything you wouldn't do. Isn't that the kind of leader you want to be?"

"How did I get so lucky to find you?" Sam smiled and kissed her.

"Must have been fate." Katrina smiled. "Dinner?"

"Yes. Steak and lobster," Sam said. The phone on her desk rang. "Hello? Yes. Thank you." She put her holster, gun, and suit jacket back on. "Ready?"

"Yes."

They opened the door and Caleb ran over.

"Commander, I want to see your office."

"Go on in, Caleb."

*****

Kimberly A. Biggerstaff © 2024

Robby and Alex met Vickers the next day at the storage unit. They went through the boxes but didn't find anything. Alex was looking through an old desk. She found a metal box and opened it. There were unsent letters inside. She opened one and read.

"He was in love with her. He wrote these letters but never sent them to her," Alex said.

"So he wanted her but maybe she didn't know."

"Jackpot! Vickers." Robby held up a rifle.

"Bag that, Officer," Vickers said, smiling. "Talk to me about motive. Why kill the airman?"

"James needed a way to get me involved with Jack again. Killing the airman drew me back to the studio and to Jack. We rekindled our romance and it kept Addy away from Jack," Alex explained.

"Sounds good to me," Vickers agreed. "But that means she didn't have anything to do with it."

Kimberly A. Biggerstaff © 2024

"Yeah," Alex said sadly and walked out to the car. She got in and just sat there. Ten minutes later Robby got in and waited.

"Talk to me, Goose," he said.

"Quoting movie lines?"

"I know you wanted to get her. Maybe she fired the weapon?"

"Doubtful. But that would be nice." She started the car. "I think the guard killed the airman to get me back into Jack's life, and Addy sent the faked photo to break us up. The guard loved Addy but she loved Jack. Do they need anything else from us?"

"Not right now," Robby said.

"Back to base," Alex said, driving.

They caught up on more paperwork. At the end of the day Alex went to Sam's office. "Come in," Sam said after Alex knocked.

"Ma'am, I have twenty-five days of leave saved up and would like to take it."

Kimberly A. Biggerstaff © 2024

"Denied," Sam said.

"But ma'am, I—"

Sam turned her computer off and stood up. "Grab your stuff and come with me," she practically ordered. They went outside and Sam asked where Alex's private car was.

"Over there, ma'am."

Sam walked to it, and Alex realized she wanted her to drive them somewhere. Sam gave her directions. They ended up at Salt Shack on the Bay.

"What are we doing here, ma'am?"

"Right now call me Sam. We're off duty." Sam ordered coconut shrimp and a beer. "You can have an adult beverage. In fact, I insist. That is if you drink."

Alex ordered a specialty cocktail.

"I know this probably isn't what you wanted," Sam said, but you need to take a breath."

"Jack may not have time. I have to get him away from her."

"Isn't there a premiere coming up?" Sam asked.

"Yes. The director invited Robby and me to it. Jack and Addy will be there."

"Got a dress yet?"

"What? No."

"Tomorrow after work we'll go shopping," Sam said.

"Shopping?"

"We'll need dresses."

"We?"

"Don't worry about it. Just trust me."

Alex shook her head. They talked for a while and had more drinks. "Well, I think we should call it a night. Or I should."

"I'll get a ride for us," Sam said.

"No, I'm okay to drive. I've been drinking water for the last half hour."

"We'll wait thirty more minutes and you can take me home. I'll have another drink," Sam told her.

Sam was a little tipsy when the half hour was up. She gave Alex the address, and when they arrived Alex was surprised. "You live here?" she said, looking at the large home. It looked as big as Jack's house.

"Yeah. Renting it. Want to come in?"

"Uh, yes."

The house was big and modern. A two-story four bedroom with a pool and spa. When they finished the tour Alex said, "I give up."

"What do you mean?"

"Nothing. It's none of my business."

"I inherited some money from my parents. I'm rich," Sam said, still a little tipsy. "You know if I weren't married—"

"Are you flirting with your troop, Samantha?" Katrina said, coming downstairs in a T-shirt. She smiled at Sam and then said, "Did you two have fun?"

"Yes," Sam said. "You'll have to take me to work in the morning. I left my car on base." Sam smiled at her and gave her a kiss. "I ever tell you what great legs you have?"

"Yes, you have," Katrina said.

"I should get home. Thank you . . . Sam."
Kimberly A. Biggerstaff © 2024

"Night," Sam said. "See you tomorrow."

*****

Sam and Alex went shopping for dresses after work the next day. "How did you get invited?" Alex asked her.

"I made a call. Katrina already has her dress. We'll be there. I don't want you to do anything stupid, okay?"

"Yes, ma'am."

"Alex?" There had been something bothering her all day, and she needed to clear the air.

"Yes, ma'am."

Sam sighed and said, "Last night, I . . . uh, my wife said I might have flirted a little. That was inappropriate, and I apologize."

Alex took a second and with watery eyes she walked over to Sam. With hurt and sadness in her voice Alex said, "You mean you didn't mean what you said? I . . . I thought we might . . ." She stopped talking and touched Sam gently on the face.

Kimberly A. Biggerstaff © 2024

At first Sam was surprised, and then she looked into Alex's eyes. "Wow, if you acted like that in your movie you should get an Academy Award."

Alex smiled and walked away. "I had you for a minute."

*****

Sam arranged a limo and picked up Robby and Alex for the premiere. The limo pulled up in front of the theater, and a man opened the door. Flashes went off from all the paparazzi, but no one knew who they were. They went inside and looked around.

"Alex, there's Ford," Robby said. Eventually Ron saw them and came over.

"Glad you could come," he said.

"Ron, this is my boss, Samantha Barrett, and her wife, Katrina Davis."

"Yes, you called my office. Nice to meet you."

"You too," Sam said.

Kimberly A. Biggerstaff © 2024

"Jack hasn't arrived yet. They'll stop over there and take photos and questions from the press. At least he's supposed to," Ron said. They took some champagne from a waiter passing by and talked about the movie.

"Here they are," Ron said.

Jack looked okay. Not as bad as when Robby or Sam last saw him. His dark hair and beard were trimmed. His tux was neat and shoes shined. But he didn't smile. He and Addy waited for their turn, and a woman guided them to their place on a special area on the carpet. Addy whispered something to Jack, and the camera flashes went off. He smiled and began speaking. Alex stepped closer to them behind the press.

"I'm Jack Hailey, owner of Hailey's Comet Studios. This is my fiancée, Addy Parker."

Alex felt her heart sink when he said Addy was his fiancée. The press asked all kinds of questions. Addy answered most of them. When they moved from the press area, Alex went back to Robby and the others.

"Robby, I want to go."
Kimberly A. Biggerstaff © 2024

"Alex. Please stay for a while," Ron said. "Maybe seeing you will help."

"He's right. Come on," Sam said.

They walked over to Jack and Addy. Jack seemed in a daze. Addy was talking to everyone. "Jack," Alex said. Addy looked at her.

"What are you doing here, Alex?" she asked.

"I was invited. Jack, are you okay?"

"Tell her, Jackson Jr."

"I'm fine. Never better."

"You're not fine, Jack. She's drugging you," Alex said.

"I'm fine. Never better," he said again.

"Hello again," Sam said. "Remember us?" She took a sip of champagne and pulled Katrina closer.

"Why the hell are you here?" Addy asked.

"I made a call. By the way, I never did formally introduce myself. Agent Samantha Barrett, Air Force OSI. Federal agent."

Kimberly A. Biggerstaff © 2024

The look on Addy's face said it all. "You! You killed James. You're a cop. You bitch." Addy slapped her.

Sam smiled and said, "Thank you. I'm arresting you for assaulting a federal agent. Alex, would you care to do the honors?" Sam pulled a pair of handcuffs from her purse and gave them to Alex.

"You can't do this. No. Jack. Jackson Jr., help me," she begged as Alex cuffed her.

"I'll take her," Robby said. "Take care of Jack."

"Katrina, you can stay if you want," Sam told her as she took Addy's purse from under her arm. "I have paperwork to do." Sam kissed her.

"Agent Barrett. Thank you," Alex said, smiling.

"Jackson Jr. is the phrase to control him. Here." She handed her a card she pulled from her purse. "That's a private hospital that will help with the addiction and the control. They're waiting for you to take him there."

"Agent Barrett, well, you clean up nice," Vickers said, looking her up and down. "What am I doing here?" Sam had called Vickers in advance and told him he should come to the premier, just in case. He arrived with two patrolmen.

"This woman assaulted me after I identified myself as a federal agent. I want to press charges. Check her purse," Sam said, handing it to him.

Vickers searched Addy's purse after putting gloves on and pulled out a vial. "Well, well. Morphine and a syringe."

"Alex, get a photo and show that to the doctors," Sam told her.

"No, no, he needs me. He loves me," Addy said. "Jack. Jackson Jr., I love you. Come with me."

"Get her out of here," Vickers told an officer. The officer took her arm from Robby. Sam followed them out.

"I love you, Addy." Jack started to follow them, but Alex stepped in front of him. She smiled at him with tears in her eyes.

"Jack. No," she said. He looked down at her. "Jackson Jr., come with me. It's me, Alex. I'm going to help you." She held her hand out.

"Alex. You're going to help me." He took her hand.

"Alex," he said as he wiped the tear away from her cheek.

"Help . . . me."

Kimberly A. Biggerstaff © 2024

EPILOGUE

Two months later

Alex went into Sam's office. "How's the packing, ma'am?

May I help?"

"Looking forward to getting rid of me, Yates?"

"Not at all, ma'am."

"Six months seems to have gone fast. How's Jack?"

"He's getting better. He has a long road ahead of him.

In case you're interested, Addy also used the drugs

scopolamine, and flunitrazepam, along with morphine. Vickers

found all kinds of drugs at her apartment. She was using

classical conditioning, as well. She really screwed him up. But

he's strong. He'll get through it."

"He's lucky to have you."

"We're lucky to have had you, ma'am," Alex said, shaking her hand. "I can't thank you enough for everything you've done. It's been an honor knowing you. I wish you could stay longer. You're a great commanding officer."

Sam shook her hand. "Thank you, Alex. You're a really good agent. You solved the case and got the guy. I'm sure I'll be reading about your cases someday." Then she smiled and said, "Just don't shoot your partner." She picked up the last box and walked out of her office. They had already given her a small going-away party the day before. but everyone stood and said goodbye again as Sam walked through the door leading outside that Robby held open for her.

"Let me take that, ma'am," Robby said, taking the box. They walked her to her car, and Robby put the box in the back seat.

"It's been a pleasure, ma'am," Alex said. Robby and Alex snapped to attention and saluted her. Sam returned the salute and got in the car and drove off.

Kimberly A. Biggerstaff © 2024

"Well, partner. We still have some open cases," Robby said.

"Yeah, let's go interview that witness." Alex handed Robby the keys.

"What's this?"

"You drive," Alex said. "I've . . . been working on it. I'm ready." She smiled at him.

*****

One year later

"Katrina? How would you like to be my plus one?" Sam asked, holding the invitation.

"Another embassy party?"

"No, it seems a certain OSI agent and movie studio owner are getting married," Sam said, smiling.

THE END

Kimberly A. Biggerstaff © 2024

www.ingramcontent.com/pod-product-compliance
Lightning Source LLC
Chambersburg PA
CBHW060922180626
46817CB00004B/1350